THE GIFT
Andy Wakefield

The journey that you take doesn't always reach the destination you intended.

Dedicated to Laura. Wherever and whoever you are now.

Chapter 1

I first met David two years after he died.

It was a summer evening and the sun was about to sink into the sea. As I went to sit down on the clifftop wooden bench I read the brass plaque attached to it. " In memory of David Roberts who loved this spot. Born September 28 1935 died August 26th 2017"

Well David, whoever you were, I can see why you liked it here, so quiet and peaceful I thought. Eighty-two when you snuffed it, no hang on you didn't quite make eighty-two. Still eighty-one isn't a bad innings really considering my old man didn't make seventy-five.

To this day I can't really say what brought me there. I just wanted to drive somewhere and the coast seemed like the best idea. I didn't want to go to the seaside drenched in fish and chips, amusement arcades, shops selling stacks of plastic buckets and spades and the smell of candyfloss and doughnuts. To me the coast is different, that's why I never call it the seaside. It's where the land stops and the sea starts without any commercial meddling and that's where I wanted to be, alone except for the occasional distant dog walker.

I suppose the real truth was that I couldn't handle the seaside as it brought back such happy memories of when I enjoyed all that shit. Watching the excitement on Charlie's face as she shoved countless coins into a dodgy glass encased mechanical crane to try and win a fluffy toy that would have cost a fraction of my money that she was spending. Followed by a trip to the crap shop by the pier to choose an inflatable rubber ring that had to be the right shade of pink. All other colours were for boys apparently. We would splash about in the surf before making sandcastles decorated with paper flags, then sit on the prom wall where I had to make sure that every single grain of sand was removed from between Charlie's toes before she would agree to have her sandals on. Eating an ice cream also came with its own set of rules, which amounted to biting the end off the bottom of a cornet and sucking the whipped white ice cream through the hole until the cornet was completely soggy.

I leant back on the bench and gazed to the left of the horizon at a dozen or so seagulls eagerly following a small fishing boat and heard a softly spoken voice to the right of me.

"Lovely evening isn't it?"

I hadn't seen the old man approach or felt him sit down beside me, which I put down to my wondering mind and preoccupation with the squawking birds. He was quite a dark-skinned man who could have been of Latin origin but without any foreign accent.

"Yes it is," I said "beautiful view as well."

"Despite the noisy neighbours," continued the old man as he pointed to the seagulls.

I smiled and looked across at him. I couldn't help noticing that he was wearing odd socks. Not by mistake it seemed but very likely to be intentional as one was bright orange the other light blue. I warmed to his slight oddness and was even prepared to continue the chat.

That was until he introduced himself.

"David Roberts's the name…that's me." He pointed to the brass plaque on the back on the bench that I was partially obscuring.

Oh shit I though, a weirdo.

The last thing I wanted at this particular time was to hear the ramblings of a sad old loony. I made my excuses and got up to leave.
"Nice to meet you David but I must make a move."

As I turned my back on the old man I heard the softly spoken voice again.
"You can talk to Charlie you know Tim, she can still hear you."

"How do you?"…

I turned to ask him how he knew my name and the name of my beautiful daughter but he had gone. How was this possible? The bench was in the middle of nowhere. I even went to the edge of the cliff, a few yards away, to look down and see if the crazy old man had jumped but the only thing squashed against the rocks below was a supermarket shopping trolley and a couple of old car tyres. But even if what had remained of him had been down there how did he know what he knew? I lived over sixty miles away and had never set foot on that part of the coast before that day.

I suddenly felt quite ill and had to sit back down on the bench again. I stared at the brass plaque and tried to make sense of what had just happened. After I had stopped trembling and the breathlessness had all but returned to normal breathing I came up with the only logical explanation. I must have fallen asleep, yes that was it, I hadn't slept well for months and being at that very peaceful place and after reading the plaque I must have dozed off and dreamt the whole thing.

I sat for a while and gazed back out to sea. The fishing boat and the seagulls had gone, or were they also in the dream? It was getting cloudy and dark and I could hear distant thunder. I walked towards my car parked at the cliff top lay-by about half a mile away, looking back a couple of times at the bench.

As I sat in my car I had a sudden stomach cramp. It made me think of the terrible pain that Charlie had gone through during the last months of her life as the vicious and aggressive cancer invaded her teenage body. Almost everything made me think of her. Seeing a menu listing her favourite food, smelling the perfume of a young woman on a tube train, which wasn't even the same smell as Charlie's perfume, passing a shop window displaying clothes that she would have loved but was never going to wear, even seeing a discarded piece of litter that she would have picked up and put in a bin as she angrily said, *"some people!"* I still couldn't listen to music. Not just the type that she loved but also any genre. Blues, dance, jazz, rock and even classical would say something that would fire a bullet into my heart. As for country…forget it.

I sometimes wondered how my ex-wife was

coping. She moved to Australia to live with her older sister because she said she just couldn't cope with the pain of living in the same country where Charlie once lived. I don't see how leaving the country could make the pain any less, but towards the end of our marriage we didn't seem to agree on very much. Even Charlie's name was a topic for disagreement. Clare would insist on calling her Charlotte and she blamed me for calling her Charlie even though Charlie preferred it to Charlotte.

I'd decided to work from home after Clare and I got divorced four years ago as it gave me more options to be with Charlie other than just every other weekend.

When Charlie became ill I would spend nearly every day with her and my marketing consultancy had to take a back seat.

The thunderstorm was now overhead and the rain bounced on the roof of my car and cascaded down the windscreen and side windows hiding me from the outside world and allowing me to cry unnoticed by any passerby.

The next two weeks was pretty much the same as the previous two, same shit different day as the saying goes.

Work was about the only thing left now so I had to re-establish contact with some of my old clients and try and drum up a few new ones as I had lost quite a lot of business during my year off. The mortgage still had to be paid and the ready meals still had to be shoved into the microwave. And that, in a nutshell, was how life was. Eat when I remembered to, drink too much and sleep too little.

Although that day at the coast kept on popping into my head I would convince myself to forget about it, but during the less sober times, usually during the second bottle of wine or a generous glass of grappa I would decide to go back the next day when I wasn't drunk. When each new day dawned however I would do what I always did, work and sometimes cry.

Every now and then something Charlie had said would come back to me. Not triggered by anything in particular but just as I was thinking about her. One day I was on my way home from picking up a few bottles of cheap wine from the supermarket when I remembered her saying *"what's going to happen to me Dad?"* It was the day she was diagnosed with stage four bowel cancer. She was seventeen. How the fuck could she have bowel cancer at seventeen? We were told it was very rare, which didn't make it any easier to accept. There was nothing I could say to her, nothing I could kiss or rub better. What use is a Dad who can't make his kid feel better?

I drove past my house and kept on driving heading for the coast where I could just sit and stare, but deep down I wanted to see David. I wanted to ask him how I could talk to her like he said I could. Even if that first meeting was just a dream, I wanted to dream again.

I arrived at the cliff top lay-by as it was starting to get dark. It was only 4pm but it was late October and the clocks had already gone back. The walk to the bench seemed longer than I remembered, maybe because of the chilly autumn air. The blue summer sea had changed to a dirty grey colour, which made me feel even colder.

As I approached the bench I had mixed feelings of why the hell am I doing this combined with not being able to get to the bench fast enough. It must be how it feels to go on a blind date – something I'd never done or ever wanted to do but here I was hoping to meet someone who didn't even exist. I didn't however think once about turning back.

I glanced at the brass plaque, sat down and stared at the murky colourless view in front of me. After a couple of minutes a robin settled a few feet away from me and started to peck away at a bald patch of earth *"Hello Robin,"* I said assuming that all robins were called Robin.

Well, there's no chance I'm going to fall asleep this time I thought except maybe from bloody hypothermia. As the robin flew away the soft-spoken voice said, *"hello Tim, good to see you again."* The coldness instantly left my body and was replaced by a rush of burning heat that filled my neck and face. How was this possible? I turned to look at the old man who was wearing the same clothes, and odd socks, as the last time.

"How have you been?"
"Bloody awful." I answered. *"And now totally confused."*
"Why?" said the old man. I still preferred to think of him as the old man and refused to accept that he was David Roberts.
"Because I thought you were a dream."
"Oh I see." Said the old man with a slight laugh in his voice.
I didn't want to challenge his existence I just wanted to know the answer to what had been nagging at me for the last few months.

"You said that I can still talk to Charlie – but how?"
"Just talk to her…simple as that." The old man replied.
"But she can't answer me."
"Neither can that bird that you spoke to a few minutes ago." Said the old man with a slightly annoying knowing look.
"I only said hello and anyway Charlie has gone she doesn't exist any more." The words sounded harsh as I said them.
"How do you know that she doesn't exist?"
"Because she's dead." I shouted, forcing a tear to run down my cheek and into the corner of my nouth.

"Do you remember the last time you came here and that bush over there was full of flowers?"
"Why are you changing the subject?" I said. The old man continued without answering my question.
"Where are the flowers now?"
"It's autumn, they died and they've gone."
"Have they?" said the old man. *"And what will happen next spring?"*
"They'll be back, of course." I answered sharply.
He looked at me, smiled and said, *"no they won't, they will be different flowers, similar to this year's but not the same ones. They will have their own unique shape and colour but they will come from the same bush. Nothing ever dies it just gets reborn. The bush is like the spirit that keeps on reproducing"*

I was starting to see the point that he was making.
"You mean reincarnation?"
"If that's what you want to call it."
"So what would you call it?" I asked.
"Reality." He said. *"It's what really happens."*

I told him that I didn't believe in that sort of stuff. I always needed evidence before I believed in anything. Something concrete that I can see and touch, but as I told him this I also doubted myself about my own beliefs. If he really is or was David Roberts how can I be having an intense conversation with a dead man?

The old man changed the subject again.
"You have to let go Tim."
"I can never let go of Charlie," I said, *"never."*
"I don't mean Charlie. You've got to let go of yourself."
I looked away for a second and when I looked back at him he had gone again without telling me how I could talk to Charlie. Maybe I shouldn't have doubted the reincarnation thing and just gone along with it.

I walked back to the lay-by and another thought crossed my mind. I was dreaming again but this time I was at home and soon I'll wake up and all will be explained. But I didn't wake up. Instead I carried on walking, past my car and on to the small village another quarter of a mile away. Maybe there I will find out more about the mysterious David Roberts. I'd tried to Google him a few weeks before but there were hundreds of David Roberts and none of them were in this remote part of England.

The village was even smaller than it looked from the road. I went into the tiny pub that served the dozen or so surrounding houses and whatever local farms were nearby.

The landlord was a man of about my age and at least twice my size widthwise.
"Evening, what can I get you?" He said in a cheery high-pitched voice.
"Half a pint of your best local stuff please."

Looking around the small room there were three old men sipping pints at a corner table. And that was it apart from a grey-faced old mongrel asleep by their feet. The landlord passed me my drink.
"What brings you here? Let me guess, you're lost." He said with a laugh in his voice. An idea came to me, which hopefully would enable me to gain the information I wanted.

"No," I answered, *"I'm doing a book. I'm a*

photographer and writer. I'm interested in local people whose names are preserved on benches throughout England. I want to bring them back to life by telling their stories."
Brilliant, I thought. How did I manage that on the spur of the moment?

"Sounds interesting," said the landlord, *"found any good ones?"*
As I was on a roll I continued to expand on my fictitious project.
"Certainly have, I've found a Spitfire pilot, a woman who fostered over fifty children and a composer, amongst many others."
"Fantastic," said the landlord. *"And they've all got their names on benches you say?*
"Yes either in parks, in woods or overlooking the coast. Places where they just loved to be – their favourite spots. One that I'm interested in knowing more about around here is on the coastal path about a mile away. David Roberts his name was. Ever heard of him?"
"Heard of him but didn't really know him. He didn't live in the village. Lived a bit further down from here in a farm workers cottage. Ben over there knew him. He'll be able to help you."

One of the old men with Dickensian mutton chop sideburns, that mister Bumble would have been proud of, turned to face me.
"Now what have I done?" said Ben.
I sat down with the three men, ordered them a refill and told them the same story that I had told to the landlord.

"Ah old David odd socks. Don't know who coined the nickname but I think it came from that film 'Dances with wolves' which had a wolf called Two Socks because David always wore odd socks– sort of his trademark it was."

Ben had delivered the first cold shiver down my back but it was about to get a lot more chilling.

Ben went on to tell me that David was born in the east end of London and was evacuated during the war with his mother who died of TB during their time as evacuees and his father was killed on a merchant ship that was torpedoed. David spent the next ten years in and out of orphanages. He ended up as a carpenter – a bloody good one according to Ben and sometimes they worked together as Ben used to be a bricklayer.

"He was a kindhearted fella. Always helped those who needed help." Said Ben. *"He was also something of a hero as he saved a little girl from drowning,"* Ben continued. *"Little girl of about seven she was. Her mum was watching her playing by the shoreline when she dozed off. The kid must have wandered out a bit and got into trouble. Luckily old odd socks was walking along the beach and ran into the water to rescue her...gave her the kiss of life as well. Gordon here saw it all didn't you Gord?"*

Another of the men spoke up.
"Certainly did, I was walking old Molly here," Gordon pointed to the dog, *"When I heard all this kerfuffle going on. David was trying to bring the little girl round and her Mum was hysterical shouting Charlotte! Charlotte! The little girl gave a cough and a splutter and all seemed well, thank goodness."*

I couldn't believe what I had just heard. My brain went into overdrive trying to work out if this was coincidence or was it my Charlie. I remembered when she was just about to turn seven, I was in South Africa on business for almost a month, but if it was Charlie why didn't I know about it from Clare or even Charlie herself?

I knew I had to contact Clare but I wasn't sure if I really wanted to know the truth. After all, if this bizarre story was true how could Charlie have managed to keep it from me? It was going to be difficult, as Clare and me had barely spoken since the funeral. Rather than call out of the blue I sent her a text saying that I needed to talk to her. As expected I didn't get an instant reply. It arrived the following day.
"OK call me tomorrow midday your time"

Twelve o'clock came around and I poured myself a large glass of red.
"Hi, how are you keeping?
"About as good as you are I would guess."
Said Clare in her official voice.
"How's Australia?" I asked.
"What is it that you wanted Tim?"
"When Charlotte was about seven did you ever take her to a place called Lee Bay Beach?"
There was a silence and I thought that she had hung up.
"Clare?"
"I'm still here. So you've been doing some

spying. What do you know?"

I didn't tell her the whole story. As well as having no desire to I still didn't believe it myself. I just said that I was in the area coming back from a business trip and stopped in a local pub and got talking to a few locals who told me about a bit of a drama they had there about ten years ago involving a little girl and a local hero.

There was a silence again before Clare spoke, this time with a little less aggression in her voice.
"Well I don't believe you for a minute how you found out but yes it is true."
I asked her why had she not told me. She gave me an answer that didn't come as a total surprise. She said that at the time we weren't exactly soul mates, in fact I was being an absolute bastard and she just wouldn't have been able to handle the way I would have reacted. Especially as she knew I would question how it happened and discover that it was her fault. She had told Charlie not to tell me, as it would have upset me too much and best that it remained their secret.

Without telling Clare that I knew the answer to my question I asked if she knew the name of the man who had saved Charlie. She said it was an elderly man called David who had since died. Apparently she had kept in touch with him over the years and was told about his death by a woman who lived close by to David in a place called Hill Farm.

"So now you know," said Clare.
I certainly did – I knew that it really was Charlie who nearly drowned, I knew that David Roberts really did exist, and I knew that I was an absolute bastard as a husband and probably still was an arsehole of a person.

Two questions still remained unanswered. Could David Roberts have faked his own death and still be alive and if so, how did he know me?

One thing was obvious; I had to meet the woman at Hill Farm.

About a ten-minute walk from the cliff-top there was a short gravel drive that led to a stone farmhouse surrounded by a few outbuildings and all the usual, accompanying farm type smells.

As I drove up to the house I was greeted by a couple of barking border collies. A middle-aged woman appeared from one of the out buildings praising the dogs for the alert. I wound down my window and introduced myself.
"Hello, my name's Tim Wade, could you spare me a couple of minutes please?
"Depends on what you're selling." Said the woman cautiously.

I told the woman some of my story but didn't mention my strange encounters at the cliff-top bench. The woman wiped her hand on her John Deere farmers overalls, shook my hand and introduced herself as Helen.

After explaining to Helen why I'd only just found out about what happened at the beach all those years ago she said how she had met my ex-wife when she was visiting David on his birthday a year after he had saved Charlie's life. They seemed to have got on quite well. Helen had never met Charlie though; Clare had always come on her own. I doubt if Charlie ever knew that her mum used to visit David

24

from time to time.

I told Helen that the reason I had come to see her was to find out a bit more about David. What I didn't tell her was I wanted to know if he was really dead. I felt a bit guilty about all the probing I was doing because I could see that Helen thought David was a wonderful man. She even said that he put the gentle in gentleman. He would do all sorts of jobs at the farm after Helen became widowed and he never took any payment for it, except for the occasional meal and an evening walk along the cliff top. That was when I discovered that it was Helen who had the bench and plaque put there. She said, *"there was never any sort of, you know, thing going on between us. We were just good friends."*

Helen told me that she had found David late one evening. He was due to come to her that day to repair some fencing but didn't turn up, which was, as she said, very unusual for David. She couldn't contact him because he didn't have a phone. *"Never had any use for one,"* she said.
"So, I walked over to his cottage, knocked on the door but there was no answer. The door

wasn't locked so I went in and found him slumped in a chair. Postmortem said it was a massive heart attack."

So, there was a post mortem I thought, well that kind of squashes the idea of him still being alive but not to finally give up on the theory I asked Helen if she had any pictures of David as I never got to meet him. *"Got one in my bag,"* she said. Sure enough it was the same David, a full-length picture of him wearing odd socks. *"He was quite a spiritual man, probably got that from his mother who was Indian,"* said Helen.

Was it at all possible that David had some sort of spiritual quality that has enabled him to incarnate and could this piece of information start to elucidate the perplexity that was fucking up my life?

I had to see him again.

This time I didn't go home to mull things over. There was nothing that needed mulling. I felt a sense of relief that I hadn't been dreaming and that maybe I wasn't crazy after all. The evidence was there, I really did have two encounters with a dead man and what really made me feel sick with excitement was if he could reappear could Charlie? Maybe it was a naïve notion but I had to find out. Little did I know at the time that this would be the start of my long and enriching, although arduous, journey.

I drove down to the lay-by to start my walk to David's bench. As I made my way up the rugged path I started to wonder what David used to think as he walked from his tiny cottage to the place where he loved to sit. Would he meditate or just take in the view? Was he secretly in love with Helen but too shy to let his feeling known or was he just a nice but lonely man? All of this and more seemed important now that I was beginning to let go of my preconceptions. Then I remembered the last thing that David had said to me, *"You've got to let go of yourself."* That's what he must have meant. I must stop doubting what I don't understand and open my mind. Only then will I be able to talk to Charlie.

It was too dark to see the bench, which was now only a few yards away but I did see a tiny red light. I could smell the musky aroma of weed and could hear distant voices. As I got closer I saw two teenage boys. One of them was sitting on the back of the bench carving something into it with a knife. The other was standing next to him taking a long drag on a spliff.

I felt angry that both David's bench and my own anticipation were being defaced. I shouted at them to fuck off, which they did without any hesitation, dropping both the joint and the knife as they fled.

I stamped on the glowing, stubby cigarette and shouted, *"bastards"* as I threw the knife over the cliff. Sitting down I felt my heart pounding with rage. The thought of what I might have done to them or what they would have done to me if they had decided not to run off scared me.

I looked at the thoughtless damage the word 'Kev', that was freshly carved into the bench, had done. I grabbed a handful of dirt and rubbed it into the letters to try and make them less prominent.

As I sat and looked at a few stars visible

through the part cloudy sky I eventually began to question my anger at the two boys who were merely enjoying a little stimulation and leaving their mark on an old wooden bench.

I became aware of David, even before he said, *"Hello Tim."*
"Hello David, I think I owe you an apology for doubting you."
"You owe yourself an apology for doubting yourself," said David smiling.
"I know you saved Charlie's life when she was a little kid," I said *"Is that why I'm here and able to speak to you? Did you, somehow, get me to come here all along? Because I can't explain why I came here that first time back in summer. I thought I just wanted to drive to the coast but why here? The more I try to work any of this out the more confusing it seems to get"*

What happened next almost rendered me unconscious.

It was if David was holding my hand, which he clearly wasn't, as he said.
"The day my mother died was exactly the same second that your daughter was born and my

mother's spirit continued on, which I didn't know at the time…until…that day, seven years later, when I breathed life into your daughter. In the short time that Charlie wasn't breathing my mother was speaking to me."
"What did she say? Did she know that Charlie was going to die of cancer?"

David looked at me and said nothing for a few seconds, which seemed to calm me down as I looked into the eyes of someone who looked very much alive. Then he spoke again.
"Everything will become clear in time."

"So where do we go from here?" I asked.
"Not we, you, there is a lot for you to do when you have The Inner Sight."
"What's the Inner Sight?" I asked.
"You'll know exactly what I mean when you have it," answered David smiling
"All I want David is to be able to talk to Charlie."
"Everything that you think you want now will change in the future."

I looked at David – there was no aura or spiritual glow around him. I didn't want to touch him to see if my hand would go straight

30

through as that would have been another demonstration of disbelief and that was something that I didn't have any more.

I asked him again to explain what he meant by the 'Inner Sight'
"All in good time Tim, first you have to go to Narad Ghat."
"Where's that?" I asked.
"India," he answered without batting a deceased's eyelid.
"To do what?" I asked.
"To learn and not to question," replied David. *"Just go."*

And with that he was gone.

Chapter 2

Back home and with a large glass of wine to hand I discovered, from the Internet, that Narad Ghat was a religious Hindu place on the banks of the river Ganges. The nearest airport was Varanasi and involved a two-flight change, fifteen-hour journey. I booked a one-way ticket – something that I'd never done in my life before and took a large gulp of alcohol.

Two days later I was sitting on a plane heading for who knows what?
I avoided making any conversation with anyone in case they asked me where I was going and why – answers to which I didn't have a clue. All I did know for sure was I would piss off my last remaining clients and see my business go down the toilet. What made the reality worse was that it was me who was flushing it away after a career of fighting

to keep the customer happy and over delivering, which I didn't really need to do as my Dad, who I had never really got on with in his later life, had left me a small fortune, which meant that I didn't have to work at all for the rest of my life but pride kept me working and paying my own mortgage and the money stayed invested, earning even more money.

I could have quite easily retired after Dad died and enjoyed a comfortable life, but a strange sort of guilt had stopped me from doing that – until that day when I decided to buy a one-way ticket to India.

After all I could meet a beautiful Indian woman who made curries to die for and I would live a happily ever after Bollywood lifestyle dressed in a white silk caftan and curly shoes. But clutching at those ridiculous straws soon made my thoughts return to Charlie, the bizarre connection with her and David's mother and what was waiting for me over five thousand miles away.

I arrived at Varanasi airport in heat that was like walking into a furnace.

Eventually, after a very slow, casual process of clearing Indian customs and locating my bag I took a beaten-up old Hindustan Ambassador taxi to Narad Ghat.

Air conditioning didn't exist in this relic and what hit me straight away, as I wound down the window, were smells that you could taste, in both a good and bad way. Spices, incense, flora, urine and garbage. Without the good smells the bad would have been pretty unbearable or rank as Charlie would have said. Rudyard Kipling was certainly right when he said, *"The first condition of understanding a foreign country is to smell it."*

The bad smells however were a small price to pay as I was rewarded with colour. It was as if, up until now, I had lived my life in black and white. The colours of India are intense, vibrant and entrenched in its awareness. Colour is how India tells its story and each colour holds an important cultural, religious and traditional meaning.

Blue is the colour of peace and serenity and represents infinity like the sky and the ocean. Krishna, the god of compassion, tenderness and love in Hinduism is also depicted in blue. Wearing blue is believed to have a calming effect.

Yellow is sacred and symbolises the balance of life, sharing the same healing qualities as the sun, emanating warmth, optimism and light. Yellow is worn to celebrate the Hindu festival of the coming of spring and the goddess Saraswati wears a yellow dress and yellow sweets and saffron rice are eaten.

Red represents fertility and opulence. The red tilak, a red mark placed on the forehead, is used across India as a ritual mark of welcome. The tilak symbolises the third eye of the Lord Shiva and is believed to protect the inner wisdom of those who display it.

White is the colour of calm, which represents serenity and spreads the message of peace. It is the colour from which all other colours emerge, and so stands for purity. The main shades of white are represented in nature by the August moon, the conch shell, clouds when the rain has cleared and the white surf of the sea.

All of this I was completely ignorant of that first day I arrived at my destination looking like a particularly bad example of an Englishman abroad. The black jeans and denim shirt had transformed me into a human pressure cooker.

Narad Ghat was built on a series of levels, like giant steps, going down to the Ganges. Old plaster flaking, random buildings painted in terracotta and yellow crowded the vista. I sat down on one of the steps and watched a group of young women bathing, fully clothed, in the river. A few yards away from them a couple of cows were doing the same but without the clothes. Neither group seemed to bother about the dead cat that floated by.

Mixed feelings filled my head. Do I look for a clue that will help me understand why I was here? Do I try and talk to David? Or do I just give up now and book a return flight and cut my losses before all of this becomes too ridiculous to deal with? When in doubt, look at your phone I thought – no signal…bollocks!

I heard laughter and saw it was coming from some children playing by the river. The humour appeared to be mainly aimed at the funny looking pale bloke wearing strange thick clothes, sitting on the steps next to a silver suitcase. I smiled back and waved which made them laugh even more.

In the distance a figure was approaching – a tall man dressed in colourful, light robes and wearing a turban. He looked like he was in his twenties or thirties by the positive and upright way he was walking. When he got closer I could see that his face portrayed a man of at least eighty. I don't know how but I knew he was coming to see me.

I stood up as he approached me. He put his hands together in front of his face, bowed his head and said, *"Namaste Tim."*
Not wanting to look even more out of place than I already was I returned the gesture.
"Hello…how do you know me?"
Without answering my question he introduced himself.
"My name is Amar – you must be tired after your journey. Come and have some refreshment."

And with that he picked up my suitcase as if it

37

was empty and strode off up the hill like the young man that he clearly wasn't. There was nothing I could do but follow him to what would hopefully reveal the answer to the mysterious life that I was currently living.

We walked for about a mile in silence up the steep incline without any sign of heavy breathing coming from him. I on the other hand, was beginning to gasp. I could feel the sweat running down my back and into my trousers. I was wiping my brow every few yards with what was by now a completely soaked tissue that eventually just fell apart. I resorted to using my shirtsleeve, which also soon became soaked. I knew I stank worse than some of the surrounding rubbish rotting in the gutters.

At the top of the hill was an old carriage, which I later discovered was called a tonga. It had two wheels, a canvas roof and was harnessed to an old looking mule. Amar beckoned me to climb in and off we went. This was getting more bizarre by the second. I ask Amar where we were going but he just answered, *"Just enjoy the scenery Tim, it will become very beautiful very soon."*

He was right as after about half an hour the urban landscape changed to become very rural and quite kiplingesque. Mowgli and Baloo wouldn't have looked at all out of place strolling down the narrow dirt road. The journey continued for at least another two hours without much conversation, but it didn't feel like an awkward silence as the surrounding countryside provided a variety of living sounds.

Eventually we turned off the narrow road and arrived at a courtyard framed by palms, with coriander and chilies growing in large ceramic pots between the small trees. A jasmine vine, attracting masses of swallowtail butterflies, was almost covering a small house at the far end of the courtyard, it's sweet fragrance filled my head. It was like stepping into another world compared to my first introduction to the now distant Narad Ghat.

As I followed Amar's gesture to follow him into the house the aroma of Nag Champa incense took over from the Jasmine. The room was simple and very clean. Six carved wood columns, with faded turquoise paint, supported the high ceiling. Low wooden furniture, covered with large cushions, occupied most of the floor and on the walls ancient stone reliefs told stories that I was yet to understand.

Unbeknown to me, at the time, this was going to be my home for the next six years and thanks to my inherited wealth this wasn't going to give The Indian Bureau of Immigration any problems. During those years there were times when seconds seemed like hours and times when days were like seconds. Everything that I thought I knew and believed in my cocooned western world was about to change.

A young man of around late teenage wearing a white frock coat, called a kurta, entered the room. Without saying a word he handed me a large glass of water and a plate of exotic fruits. I sat down and enjoyed the best refreshments I had ever tasted; either that or it was such a welcome relief from the hot and sweaty journey to the house.

Amar sat opposite me – he smiled then eventually spoke.
"Before you begin to ask me all of the many

questions that are in your head, please listen to what I have to say."

"Okay." I said.

Amar continued. *"First of all I want to talk to you about David who you know exists but is no longer alive. So how is that possible? The answer is David's mother who you already know a little about."*

My first thought was, how the hell did he know what I knew? But that mystery seemed to pale in comparison to what was going to be revealed next as Amar paused for a few seconds to allow what he had just said to sink in before carrying on.

"Her name was Priya; she was the daughter of a maharaja, or that's what the maharaja thought until two years after the baby's birth when a servant, who was dismissed for stealing, revealed that Priya was in fact the daughter of a young man from a nearby village who Priya's mother had fallen in love with but it was a love that had to end because of the fear of reprisals by the maharaja. When the secret was made known the young man was beaten very badly and almost died. Priya and her mother were sent away. They travelled

west and eventually settled in Mumbai where Priya grew up and met David's father who was a merchant seaman.

The young man never saw his daughter. The woman he fell in love with was so ashamed of her adultery that she vowed to herself to never see him again or allow him to see his daughter. He lived alone and studied mysticism to gain insight into the true nature of our world and beyond - to be free from ignorance."

"What happened to him?" I asked.

Amar just looked at me and smiled. There was no need to interrogate him any further – I knew it was him. But how could this be possible? That would make him well over a hundred years old.

The old mystic continued to tell his story and I felt like the tightly wound ball of knotted string that had become my life, and was confusing the hell out of me, was slowly beginning to unravel.

Amar had discovered, during meditation, that

he was able to communicate with his daughter Priya during a time when she fell off a horse and lost consciousness. It was a moment when both of their real selves were detached from their bodies and able to be free to experience spiritual sight and sound even though they were miles apart. After that they discovered that they both shared a rare gift and were able to form a spiritual relationship and communicate with each other on a regular basis.

So, I know knew that Amar was David's grandfather. Surly the next thing that would be revealed was where do I fit in to all of this and why was I here? David had said that I was to gain the inner sight. Did he mean that I was going to learn telepathy or extrasensory perception? Maybe this gift that both Amar and Priya shared was given to Charlie when Priya died. After all David did say that Priya spoke to David through Charlie. But the most exciting question of all was, would I be able to communicate with Charlie?

I started to bombard Amar with all of the questions that were hurtling through my brain like an overactive pinball machine. Amar stood up and put his hand on my shoulder. Even that gentle touch seemed to work some sort of magic on me as I felt a sense of calm. *"That's enough for today – rest now and tomorrow we'll continue."* And with that he left the room. The boy reappeared and beckoned me to follow him into a simple room with a low bed and large wooden fan slowly turning above it. I thanked the boy who smiled and left me alone. The view from a small window revealed an expanse of dark distant hills lit by a full or partially full moon. There was a tranquil sound of either a stream or a fountain nearby.

My suitcase wasn't in the room but I couldn't be bothered to go and ask for it, so I just got undressed and pulled the single sheet over me. Tiredness and being unable to sleep was something that I had learned to live with and I wasn't expecting that night to be any different. The next morning I didn't even remember nodding off the night before and for a moment I thought it was still night and I hadn't yet gone to sleep but there was now light coming through the window and birds were singing.

In place of my clothes was a cream-coloured

light cotton kurta, matching pants and brown Indian slippers. There was still no sign of my suitcase just the contents of what was in my pockets, which included my passport, wallet and a few pictures of Charlie. In fact, I never saw the suitcase again or ever missed it. The new clothes were very cool and fresh on my skin as I wandered around the house feeling like I now coalesced with the surroundings. There was no sight or sound of anyone, which didn't really bother me.

Off a short corridor I came across a kitchen. Stoneware pots hung from the walls together with various ladles and spoons. There was a place set at a table with fruit juice and Idli, a soft, pillowy steamed savory cake made from rice and lentil batter. The boy appeared from outside with his hands full of freshly picked herbs. He pointed to the meal and then to me.
"Where is Amar?" I asked.
He just smiled and began to prepare the herbs. I tried again, this time in a true British approach – louder and slower.
"Amar, Am…ar?"

The boy smiled and pointed to his ears and lips and shook his head. He was either both deaf and dumb or wasn't allowed to communicate with me. I soon discovered that he couldn't hear or speak when the sound of loud squawking coming from outside didn't distract him from chopping the herbs. I looked outside and saw a kite hawk ripping a poor, colourful small bird to shreds. Even though the scene was utterly brutal it made me smile when I thought of Charlie, if she had been there, running towards the hawk shouting, *"stop it, don't be horrible you bully."*

After enjoying the healthiest breakfast that I'd ever had (my usual start to the day had been coffee, a sticky Danish and a couple of cigarettes) I went outside and sat on a rickety old bench. To call the outside a garden would have been an inadequate description. It was like a perfect jungle clearing that a Hollywood set designer couldn't have done a better job creating. A natural spring was trickling down a rock into a small pool surrounded by lilies, hostas and ferns. Sunbirds, the Indian version of hummingbirds, were hovering almost motionless as they delicately removed nectar that the flowers were offering. A gentle breeze produced a soothing melody through the taller trees, which was occasionally vocalised by distant monkeys calling for attention. Sunlight broke through sections of the jungle canopy extenuating the colours of whatever undergrowth it selected.

I spent only a few minutes thinking about things like should I have cut the grass, asked my next-door neighbour to keep an eye on the house and cancelled the Sunday papers before I had left. How could I be experiencing this amazing place with such anally retentive concerns? This was another world away from sitting in drab offices, exhaust belching cars and cold railway station waiting rooms. Much to my surprise I was beginning to feel happy in this ethereal Shangri-la. After all, what was there to go home to? Even the word home didn't accurately relate to where I merely led a day-to-day existence.

I don't remember how long I sat there – time didn't seem to be relevant anymore. I heard a softly spoken voice just at the point when I started to nod off.
"Hello Tim."
For a moment I thought it was David's voice but when I opened my eyes I saw it was Amar. He sat down beside me and smiled as he

looked at my new clothes. *"You look like a local, are you enjoying the beautiful day?"*
"Very much," I said, *"but I would love to know more about why I'm here."*
The boy appeared again with two cups of fresh mango juice.
"This is Vimal, he was abandoned because he couldn't speak or hear. I gave him the name Vimal – it means pure."

I put my hands together and bowed my head to Vimal, who did the same back with a huge grin on his face.

It was clear that Amar and Vimal could communicate – not by sign language but by, what seemed to be, some sort of telepathy. Neither of them made any hand gestures but they both seemed to know what the other was saying by looking into each other's eyes.

After a few seconds of this silent conversation Vimal left to carry on with his work and Amar turned to me and said, *"now to answer your question, you are here to receive a gift that no one has ever been enriched with before."*
I knew he wasn't about to tell me that I had won the lottery or about anything that money

could buy. The look on his face told me I was to be given something much more important.

"When certain elements are aligned, in perfect balance, amazing results are produced. Science has proved this countless times over." Amar pointed to the water trickling from the spring. *"The right amount of hydrogen aligned with the exact proportion of oxygen produces water; something that you can see, hear and taste as we all know and take for granted. Spiritualism works in the same way."*

Amar paused briefly for me to take this in. Although I nodded my head in agreement he could see the look of perplexity on my face.
"Three people have certain and different spiritual elements that, when they are aligned, will produce an understanding of life for everyone that it touches." Again Amar hesitated before continuing.
"Those three people are David, your daughter and you."

Even though I was sitting in over thirty degrees of heat a sudden coldness entered the whole of my body followed by a sick feeling in my throat. I'd had experienced panic attacks

49

in the past but this was something that had never happened to me before. Although it was physically quite unpleasant the emotional experience was very exciting. If this was a fight or flight feeling then I didn't want to either fight or run away from it.

Even before I spoke to Amar I knew anything I was about to say would sound pathetic and inept but they had to come out.
"What do you mean? How can this be true?"

Amar continued:

"David developed a deep affinity with Saṃsāra, the cycle of death and rebirth. This enabled him to experience and learn from the good and bad karma of past lives within his own unconscious mind and to apply only kindness and understanding to his own life. He was incapable of causing bad karma and could only show extreme human kindness and compassion for any living thing. This quality also tormented him throughout his conscious life as he found it difficult to understand and accept the bad karma of others. My gods and your saints have also endured this same

quality of life.

The gift that my daughter, David's mother, Priya passed to your daughter the moment she was born and Priya stopped living was the ability to transfer pure, virtuous thoughts and emotions from her own consciousness to other living things. This would have been apparent if your daughter had lived and the intensity of this gift had developed."

The moment Amar said this about Charlie, I knew it must be true. Even as a little girl she was able to comfort the most distressed animals that she had managed to rescue, either a baby bird that had fallen from its nest would live to fly away and return to visit her. Or a stray cat that would suddenly lose its fear of being lost. There were never any school bullies or scraps in the playground when Charlie was around. All of this I had taken for granted thinking that she was the perfect, happy little girl that all Dads believe about their daughters.

A spontaneous anger rush came over me that I couldn't help but direct at Amar.
"Then why did she have to fucking die?"
Amar put both of his hands on mine

transmitting an instant calmness that also made me feel ashamed of my sudden outburst.
"Your body is no part of what is really you, and indeed, your truest existence is beyond the body. The spirit has no influence over disease. It doesn't need to because the real self is always distinguished from the body and never dies."

Again I came back at Amar but this time with a bit more self-control.
"Then why can't our real self or spirit heal our own bodies from illness? Surly it must have that connection to be able to?"
Amar smiled as he answered, *"It can but most people don't know how."*
I looked at Amar and realised what he had just told me. When he said, *'most people'* he didn't mean himself.
"So you can heal yourself?" I asked.
"For as long as I need this body." He answered.
I sat back and just stared at him in awe.

"Don't you want to know about <u>your</u> gift Tim?" said Amar.
"I'm not sure I can handle it if it's anything even close to what you've just told me." I took

a sip of my cool drink as Amar continued.
"The quality you have has already been proven by your ability to communicate with David. You can connect to both the human world and the spiritual."
"Then why didn't I know this?" I questioned.
"Because your gift has been restricted by your own aspirations. Throughout your life you have followed a path that your desires and fears have laid for you - the path to success, possessions, responsibilities and competition. The further you have travelled down that path the more challenging it has been and the less intuitive you have become. Obviously you are not walking this path alone; it's a human condition that almost everyone has to protect themselves from failure and the trepidation of the unknown. When was the last time you experienced, what you call, déjà vu?"

I thought for a couple of seconds and answered somewhat awkwardly.
"Don't really know...I used to get it a lot when I was younger but it, sort of, got less and less. Suppose it's because your brain stops playing those kind of tricks on you as you get older."

Amar shook his head, *"No, it's because you*

don't allow them to happen. Those experiences like places, people and emotions that your real spiritual self wants to connect with are being rejected by you because you are overpowered by looking straight ahead on your chosen path. Your gift is to go beyond the brief occurrences of déjà vu and to connect with more enriching and prolific accomplishments as you have already experienced with your encounters with David. That is why you are here to study and become attuned with yourself for the benefit of others."

I asked him how would I do this and was he going to teach me. He said that I was to undertake six trials, the first of which would start in four days' time. Before then I was to eat and drink only what was given to me by Vimal. I also had to break contact and thoughts with my own known world. None of these instructions I found too difficult as my only source of nourishment was supplied by Vimal and as for breaking contact with the outside world, having a completely dead mobile phone determined that potential temptation.

I didn't realise at the time that those four days would be the preface to my new life story.

Every morning there were clean, identical clothes for me to wear, folded neatly at the foot of my bed, and a selection of fresh food laid out on the kitchen table. There was no sign of Amar and no point in asking Vimal where he was.

I spent the first day guiltlessly doing nothing, something I hadn't done for more years than I could remember. Back home on the rare occasions when I took a day off work there would either be future work that I needed to be planning, or having to do what I thought I was paying my accountant for. But here I was not feeling in the slightest bit errant for doing sod all.

I sat by the spring and watched the biggest dragonfly that I had ever seen dart across the rock pool and settle on one of the lilies. Maybe it was because of the huge size of the insect that I became aware of the structure of the complex design of its translucent, glassy wings and elaborate body or maybe it was the frame of mind I was in to enjoy any such distraction. As I watched this, millions of years old, flying marvel a memory popped into my head.

A few years before Charlie's death we went to my favourite place in Arizona. Charlie was fascinated by Native American culture and one day as we were watching dragonflies by a small stream in the Sedona mountains we got talking to a friendly old Yavapai-Apache woman. She told us that the dragonfly spiritually embodies the stripping away of negativity that holds us back from achieving our dreams and goals.

"They are the keeper of dreams," she said, *"the energy within that sees all of our potential and ability. Dragonflies inspire spirituality and creativity and help us on the path of discovery and enlightenment. They remind us that anything is possible."*

The old woman epitomised my feelings about Arizona. It was a place where I always felt chilled and completely free from everything that stressed me out back home. Thoughts of work, the mortgage and the bank manager would fade away as soon as I arrived in the most beautiful desert in the world. It was my utopia and way before the thought of reincarnation ever entered my head it was as though I belonged there. Some time after Charlie's death I went back to try and regain those feeling of peacefulness, but it didn't go according to plan as all I managed to do was take my grief with me and amplify it. The desert seemed cold and the tranquility wasn't there anymore. My Nirvana had disappeared.

Back in the present world so had my dragonfly, but I felt rewarded by its brief acquaintance and the fond memory of happy times.

It wasn't until the second day that I discovered the book.

It must have been there, in my room, all the time but I hadn't paid any attention to it. It was the only book in the room, in fact there wasn't much in the room at all except for a few small statues and a couple of old paintings on wood of, what I assumed were, Hindu gods. The book, which was as thick as a double helping of War and Peace, was in a small alcove next to one of the statues - a stone figure of Ganesha, the elephant-headed god of good fortune and the remover of obstacles, as I later discovered.

The cover looked ancient and was made from a thick, dark fabric. I was intrigued by its lack of design except for a few words in Sanskrit. Despite not expecting to be able to read the book I opened it anyway. The first page was another block of primitively printed Sanskrit but handwritten beside it was something that I wasn't expecting - a translation in English.

All that I have to learn is within me

Assuming that the translation had been written for my benefit I carried on turning the pages. The rest of the book however was in Sanskrit only, each page displaying, what was to me, indecipherable typography.

I was yet to discover that the rest of the translations were to be revealed to me throughout my six trials.

The next two days I spent walking and sitting in the garden with no walls.
The further I walked the more the jungle became denser and a little too unpredictable for my liking. The thought of something that

could eat me kept me within easy running distance to the house.

It didn't occur to me to venture out to find a town, a bar or any other sign of life. Although Vimal and I couldn't really communicate his presence and constant smile was all the company I needed. There was still no sign of Amar, which didn't bother me, as I knew he would return at some point. I felt as happy as I had been for ages in that place and sometimes it felt like I had been there before. Two things were puzzling me though; why did I keep getting these feelings of, what I used to call, déjà vu and what was the significance of the Sanskrit message: "All that I have to learn is within me?"

Trial 1 – Darkness

On the fifth morning Amar returned to the house. I didn't ask him where he had been and he didn't ask me what I had been doing for the last four days. I did want to know about the book though and asked him, *"Can you tell me about this? There is one translation that I assume is meant for me?"*

Amar answered in his usual gentle demeanour.
"Everyone has a spiritual guide – the book will be yours until you are ready to meet your lifelong guide. It was written by many ancient gurus who will assist you on your journey as the translations are revealed."
I pointed to the title on the front cover and asked what it meant.
"The closest it can be interpreted is 'The awakening of senses' but it means a lot more than can justifiably be translated as you will discover," he said.

The questions that immediately sprang to mind were: when will I be able to read more of the book and who will be writing the translations during my, so-called, journey? Both questions I didn't ask however as by now it was pretty clear that everything that was happening to me had its time and place to be divulged.

Although by now nothing should have taken me by surprise what happened next certainly did. Amar presented me with, what can only be described as, an elaborate human size falcon hood that would only allow me to eat, drink and breathe for, what would turn out to be, a period of six months. In other words, I was going to be blind.

Amar gently placed the hood over my head and secured the hemp laces at the back. Of course I could have, with some degree of effort, been able to pull the hood off if I had wanted to but by now I had become a somewhat zealous student prepared to suffer a teeny bit of affliction to achieve whatever mystique and rewards lie ahead.

I spent the first couple of weeks stumbling around in complete darkness, not knowing day from night due to the blackout of the hood. I slept when I was tired, which could well have been in the middle of the day, and ate when I found food on the table. The only thing I managed to achieve was a large collection of cuts and bruises bumping into various obstacles like doors, walls and Vimal who happened to be carrying something heavy or pointed at the time. Although I was unable to see his apologetic grin the thought of it would make me laugh. The opening lyrics to the song 'Handbags and glad rags' would continually nag at me; 'Ever seen a blind man cross the road trying to make the other side?' These words summed up my clumsy attempt at blindness.

As the days went by, I was able find my way around by counting my steps between each potential bump or laceration. Vimal armed himself with a tiny bell that he would ring if I was heading in his direction and after a bit of practice I could make my way around the house and garden at quite a respectable speed.

It wasn't until a while later that I began to discover, through my blindness, an amazing alternative to my lack of sight. I'd heard before that blind people have a heighten sense of smell and hearing, which I was also experiencing but the incredible thing was I started to be aware of an energy of any living thing around me, whether human or animal. As well as being able to feel their presence I knew exactly how far away they were from me and even how big or small they were. I first experienced this new sense when I was sitting in the garden listening to all that nature had to offer. I counted eight different songbirds; each one promoting its own individual call that produced a harmony with their fellow vocalists. Crickets and the occasional sound of a distant monkey completed the ensemble. As I sat back and enjoyed the rich jungle smells I became aware of a force approaching me. The energy that I was sensing didn't feel at all threatening, in fact it felt very friendly and calm as it became stronger and larger. Eager to see what it was I went to pull off my hood but stopped myself as I felt a touch on my shoulder followed by a cup being placed in my hand. It was just Vimal being his usual gracious self bringing me a cool drink.

Excited by this extraordinary discovery I spent hours practicing and refining my new talent. Within a couple of weeks I was even able to feel the energy transmitted by birds and small animals that would visit the garden. I would slowly move my hooded head scanning for any energy that I could detect. If blind man's buff had been an Olympic event, I would have won a gold medal. Occasionally, just to test my prowess, I would go in search of Vimal scouting the house and garden until I could feel his distant energy getting stronger as I got closer. I would then finally reach out and touch him, which would result in a round of applause from Vimal, and I assume one of his characteristic grins.

Every source of energy had its own distinctive characteristic. As well as their airborne position birds would be light and ethereal whereas what I assumed to be a lizard or a snake would feel heavier and cooler.

The highlight of my newly acquired mojo happened when I was walking slowly around the garden one day searching for fresh energy sensations. Even with my hood on I knew day was changing to night as the soprano of songbirds was changing to a baritone of owls and croaking frogs. I suddenly started to feel excited and extremely happy. I knew it wasn't my own energy that I was experiencing but something in the distance. It became stronger as it got closer until it felt like, what I could only describe as, a tsunami of inspirational energy heading towards me. My own energy seemed to reach out to this far more intense source, which was now close by. I called out, *"hello Amar, is that you?"*
"Yes Tim," came the reply.
I was now totally convinced that I had complete faith and trust in this man.

Amar gently put his hands around my neck and removed the hood.

The evening air had enough of a slight chill for Vimal to light a fire and make all three of us some chai. I enthusiastically told Amar about my newly found awareness, which he didn't appear to be at all surprised at but politely listened all the same. As I spoke I noticed Amar was communicating my story telepathically to Vimal who responded with his usual enthusiastic smiles and clapping.

During the next few hours of sharing the company of these two engaging men, who now seemed far less distant from my own world, I discovered the touching story of Vimal's life, through Amar's translation. The young man's eyes would fill with tears and then with laughter as he expressed to Amar the story he wanted to tell me.

Vimal was born in a village called Jamunipur, about seventy miles from Amar's house. His mother had died in childbirth and when his father discovered that his son was deaf and dumb he left him in a small temple outside of the village. This was where Amar had found

Vimal a few days later and had given him a home and a name. When Vimal reached early teenage he wanted to go back to his village to try and find his father to tell him he was happy and that he didn't blame him for being abandoned but he discovered, from someone in the village, that his father had drowned in the Tamasa River only a week after he had abandoned Vimal. It was thought that he had killed himself.

Vimal blamed himself for the death of his father believing that if he hadn't been born the way he was his father would never have abandoned him and then taken his own life. Vimal's eyes filled with tears again as Amar held the young man's hands and finished Vimal's story in his own words.
"Don't ever discount the wonder of your tears. They can be healing waters and a stream of joy. Sometimes they are the best words the heart can speak."

After spending all those months being blind I found myself still counting how many steps it was back to my room. Acting on impulse I reached for the book. There was another hand-written translation beside the next Sanskrit.

Close your eyes in order to see. The Darker the night, the brighter the stars

I felt very privileged to be able to feel what we can't always see and wondered if I would be able to experience my new sense with eyes wide open. I didn't have to wait long. I felt a tiny source of energy enter the room and fly above my head. I looked up to see a moth heading for the candle. I blew it out before the kamikaze insect hit the flame then I slept until dawn's early light woke me.

Trial 2 – Faith

I stood naked staring at the clothes at the foot of my bed. I'd taken for granted that I would slip into the usual clean, simple cotton kurta suit that was laid out for me every day. In its place was an elaborate silk tunic with intricate embroidery and a pair of, what I could only describe as, Aladdin pants. The usual slippers had also been replaced with white and gold satin shoes that wouldn't have looked out of place at a Rajah's wedding. As I thought it best not to frighten the life out of Vimal by turning up stark naked for breakfast I donned the princely outfit and made my way to the kitchen. Vimal greeted me with a slightly lower than usual bow of his head and a massive grin, even for him. I must say that the clothes made me feel terrific. Confidence was emanating from every ornate stitch of my new clothes.

Amar was sitting at the table sipping his liquid breakfast; it was very rare to ever see him eat anything.
"Good morning Tim, pleased to see you have dressed for breakfast."
"I didn't have any choice but I must say that I could get used to this."
Amar smiled, *"How do the clothes make you feel?"*
"I suppose, in a word, confident."
"That's a good start", said Amar *"as that's exactly how you need to feel. Not just because of what you're wearing but how you will believe in yourself and your abilities to enable you to communicate that belief and confidence to others."*

It was pretty obvious that I was about to embark on the next course of my education to enable me to graduate as a fully qualified something or other. Whatever it was I hoped I would be able to do it in my new chic outfit. I soon found out that wasn't to be as after my short spell of posh status I was back in the familiar cream kurta get-up at the request of Amar.

After a quick change and one of Vimal's delicious breakfasts Amar beckoned me to follow him outside. About a quarter of a mile into the jungle we came across a rope tied between two trees about two feet off the ground. I wasn't sure whether I was about to be asked to jump over it or limbo under it but Amar soon resolved my curious mind as he leapt onto the rope and sauntered across to the other side as if there wasn't a rope there at all and without stretching out his arms to balance. Still standing on the rope he turned round and called back to me.
"Your turn Tim."
"I'm willing to try," I answered, *"but I can't promise it's going to be with much panache."*

After a few failed attempts to even step onto the rope I eventually started to make my wobbly way across, first with arms outstretched and then changing to a wind milling motion in the desperate attempt not to fall off, which only seemed to make matters worse. As I was running out of body parts to help correct my balance I stuck one leg out which only caused the rope to sway even more. I was now a one-legged tightrope walker, which very quickly instigated my downfall…literally.

Amar walked back along the rope and looked down at me as I dusted myself off from my ungainly but painless fall. He stepped off the rope, took off his shoes and handed them to me.
"Try these Tim, I think you will discover they make a remarkable difference."
That must have been it, I thought, he had shoes that are specially made for tightrope walking. I put the shoes on and stepped onto the rope again, this time without hardly any wobbling. Instinctively I held out my arms and started to walk. After a few steps I felt that I didn't need to balance with my arms at all and let them lower to my sides. Enjoying the experience I stopped, looked down at the shoes and then to Amar.
"These make a hell of a difference. Now I know why you found it so easy."

The more I walked the easier and more fun it became. If I had owned shoes like these when I was a kid I could have run away and joined the circus. After a few more goes I walked back along the rope and jumped off beside Amar who smiled and asked: *"How did you find the placebo shoes Tim?"*
"What? You mean they're not tightrope walking shoes?"
"No more than your own shoes."
I was stunned for a few seconds before bursting out laughing. I'd never been so pleased about being completely duped.

"Try it again without any shoes at all." said Amar pointing to the rope.
How could I resist such a challenge? I was an accomplished high wire walker now, well maybe not such a high wire walker but a low wire walker nevertheless. Although the rope hurt my feet it wasn't enough to stop me from parading up and down from one tree to the other.
It was time for a few more words of wisdom from my wise old teacher.

"Remember how you felt when you tried on those fine clothes this morning? That is how

you must feel all of the time. The way you feel now is not because you have conquered your lack of balance, it's because you have conquered your lack of faith in your ability. It is a common belief that we can achieve anything that you put our minds to but very few people really believe it."

Not only did I feel enlightened yet again by Amar's incredible erudite wisdom, but I also thought if that was my second trial completed bring on the third; this is going to be a doddle. How wrong I was. My second trial was far from being completed; in fact it had only just begun. Walking along a rope a couple of feet above the ground was just a toe in the shallow end compared to the depths I was about to be plunged into.

Amar led me further than I had ever been into the jungle. After about an hour of walking the jungle become more like a forest with less undergrowth to hack through. Looking up, the sky could easily be seen through the tops of the trees. I became aware of an energy ahead that I had never experienced before together with the familiar energy of Vimal. Concerned that he may be in danger of being attacked by

a wild animal I told Amar what I had sensed. He smiled and answered.
"That's very good that you know Tim but don't worry we're nearly there."

Eventually in the distance I could see Vimal holding one end of a halter rope. On the other end was the other powerful source of energy that I had sensed, a stunning looking black horse with a beautiful long, thick mane, which was moving as if in slow motion in the gentle breeze. I don't think I'd ever seen such a stunning looking animal. Amar approached the horse and put his hand gently on its neck. The horse responded by nudging Amar's arm and making a soft snorting sound like the equine version of a cat purring.
"This is Bandhu," said Amar. *"The name means friend."*
Well that was good to know, I thought, as Bandhu's presence was obviously something to do with what was next in store for me.
"He will take you on your next journey."
This immediately filled me with a certain amount of trepidation as my experience of horsemanship ranged from donkey rides on Bridlington beach when I was about five to hanging on to an excited Charlie on a

fairground carousel horse. The closest I'd ever got to the real thing was shoveling garden centre horse manure onto the vegetable patch.

"Exactly what, where and when is my next journey?" I asked.

"The purpose of your journey is to gain faith in yourself and your ability to confront and prevail over obstacles beyond what you have experienced in the past. Only then will you be able to face greater challenges in the future. Your journey, with Bandhu, will be over one thousand miles from here to the Myanmar Gate at Igatpuri and will start now."

I reminded Amar again about my lack of riding experience, but it didn't seem to affect his decision to send me off into the unknown. Instead, he reached into an embroidered Jhola shoulder bag he was carrying and pulled out two pots of coloured paste, one white and the other purple. Dipping his fingers into the pots he decorated my forehead with a Tilaka, an intricate design that reached beyond the bridge of my nose.
"Don't wash this off as you will need to be recognised. It will help you along the way."

I wondered, but didn't ask, who would need to recognise me and how the mark would help me on my journey.

He then gave me a beautifully engraved antique compass and told me to travel southwest. I'd never heard of the Myanmar Gate or even Igatpuri but I asked the question anyway.
"What am I to do when I get there?"
"All will be made clear to you." Answered Amar. *"Believe in yourself, call on what you have learnt and trust Bandhu."*
Trust a horse for over a thousand miles I thought – one thing I did know about my equine travel companion was his brain was much smaller than mine. In fact on a brain to body mass ratio Bandhu's brain was about equal to a squirrel.

Regardless of this useless piece of knowledge I climbed aboard and headed southwest. I was soon to learn that my travelling companion was a lot more intuitive than I initially gave him credit for.

Bandhu was very forgiving of my initial tight grip on the reins and my flapping legs. It

wasn't until I reflected back on my earlier tightrope walk and Amar's words of *"believe in yourself"* that I started to relax. Why shouldn't I be able to do this I thought? I began to feel the energy beneath me. Amar was right; I felt an amazing sense of giving coming from Bandhu. He just wanted to please me and I felt reassured to have him there. My position became more upright, I relaxed my firm grip on the reins and my legs became motionless as they caressed the gentle giant's sides. After about half a mile I lightly wiggled my fingers on the reins to, for want of a better word, talk to Bandhu's mouth. I squeezed my legs against him and he started to trot.
"Good boy." I said to Bandhu and wished I could have said it in Hindu.
We had established a language to communicate - my body and his had become our voices.

I didn't know how I knew how to do all this; maybe it was because my great grandfather had served in the cavalry and it was in my genes. After all that had happened to me so far I was open to accept just about anything.

After a few more miles Bandhu would respond to me asking for walk trot and halt by thinking what I wanted from him combined with very subtle body signals. My confidence was growing and I knew that he was feeling it too. As we reached an open grassland area I felt him asking me to run. I sat back in the saddle, squeezed gently with my legs and let him go. In an instant we were cantering. It was a bit scary at first so I hung on to his mane to steady myself, but excitement soon conquered fear and as I let go of his mane and patted his neck he dropped his head and went into a gallop. Up until that moment I thought that being on the terraces at the Emirates ground watching Arsenal score the winning goal was the ultimate high but this was something else. My only disappointment was that I wish I could have ridden with Charlie.

It was all going so well and maybe not as much as a trial as I thought it was going to be, but what lay ahead would turn out to be a whole new venture entirely, starting with a baptism of fire…literally.

India always smelled of heat but this was different. There was an odour of burning in the air and it was getting stronger. Bandhu was aware of it too and started snorting and nodding his head. I felt a tension in his body that was being transferred to mine. After a few more nervous minutes I could see a red glow in the sky ahead. It was obvious that it was no campfire or barbeque; this was a lot larger and more serious. I convinced myself that all was under control ahead – maybe local crop control or something similar so I, somewhat apprehensively, continued on. It wasn't long before my decision proved to be the wrong one as the red sky ahead was now circling around me; it was too late to turn back.

My main concern was to communicate to Bandhu that all was OK and for him to take his confidence from me. I was sitting on a flight animal whose natural instinct was to get the fuck out of there. That last thing I wanted was for him to dump me off or to run into the circling fire ahead with me on him. I could now see the flames of what was a forest fire. Small animals were hopelessly running from the fire, some already had burn marks on their fur. The heat was now getting intense and all I could see was flames and smoke all around me.

Then about a hundred yards ahead I saw a shimmering mirage type of manifestation, like a red-hot glowing liquid on the ground. As I got closer I realised that the fire was being reflected in a lake. If I could persuade Bandhu to take the plunge we may just survive. I tweaked the reins and pushed him on with my legs. Bandhu responded and waded into the lake until we were saddle high in water. And that's where we stayed for over an hour while the fire taunted us from all sides. As the air became hotter I reached down to scoop water up onto Bandhu's neck and my face. The minutes that seemed like hours ticked away and we could both feel the water getting warmer. Although the heat and smoke was filling our lungs, from the wildfire raging around us, I felt that we were cheating the threat of death by standing in the forbidden path of the flames.

Eventually the fire was behind us. Staying in the water we walked around the perimeter of the lake until we reached the other side then made our way across the black scorched land. Bandhu picked his route around the smoldering logs and hot rocks selecting the softer burnt earth to carefully place his feet. All around us were the charred bodies of animals that had failed in their attempts to escape the inferno; black distorted bodies that had become difficult to distinguish their species.

We continued our journey slowly and cautiously, still feeling the heat rising up from beneath us. After a couple of miles we arrived at a small village. There was almost nothing left of it. The bamboo structures and thatched roofs were just piles of ash and there was a mass of the villagers' dead animals stacked in a large, tangled heap.

But that wasn't the only tragedy that was on show. Covered by linen sheets were two bodies. One was the size of an adult and the other lying beside it was obviously a small child.

I dismounted and tied Bandhu to what remained of one of the houses. A young woman with tear tracks down her blackened cheeks approached me. She had a petite build with a single plait of waist long jet-black hair and looked to be in her late twenties or early thirties. Placing her finger on the Tilaka on my forehead she asked, to my surprise in English, *"Have you been sent to help us?"*

I immediately realised what she meant. Seeing a white man displaying a Tilaka arriving on a black horse after her village had been destroyed must have appeared to be less than normal. A cold chill ran down my spine as I thought, had I been sent? Did Amar know this disaster was going to happen? Not being sure of anything anymore I answered the best I could.

"I will do all I can to help."

She said her name was Tanvi and her English had been picked up while working in a restaurant in the nearest city of Sigra but it was good enough for her to be able to explain what had happened. She told me that the fire had started in the village while honouring their Hindu custom called Dussehra, which celebrates the God Rama's victory over the evil king Ravana. Effigies are burnt to signify the victory of good over evil. Ironically a sudden wind had caused the fire to get out of control and had created a horror beyond their imagination. Most of the villagers had managed to run in the opposite direction to the wind and had taken shelter but the two who hadn't made it lay in evidence under the linen shrouds.

Still torn between thinking was this coincidence or destiny that I was here I summoned my senses to feel the energy that was present in the village. It wasn't feeling in any way promising. Everyone from the very old to small children were confused and incapable of doing anything positive. Some were looking towards the distant red angry sky, scared that the fire may return to finish off what little was left. I felt their immediate future was down to me.

The first thing I did was to take a little boy's hand and lead him to Bandhu. I stroked one of Bandhu's legs and gestured for the kid to do the same. Very soon Bandhu had attracted the attention of most of the village children and stood rock solid as they patted and stroked him. The next thing was to bury the two bodies. I grabbed a charred shovel that was leaning against a partially collapsed wall and started to dig a small grave for the dead child. As I lifted the almost weightless body a breeze blew back some of the linen sheet revealing the unrecognisable face of the child. It was impossible to see whether it was a boy or girl. I thought I was going to be sick but managed to pull the sheet back over the tiny, carbonized features and gently laid the body in the grave. Seeing my actions I was joined by two men who started to dig a grave for the other victim.

One by one the villagers mobilised themselves into action clearing away what they could of their damaged homes and disposing of their dead animals. Tanvi went to a part of the forest unaffected by the path of the fire and returned with flowers that she placed onto the two graves.

As dusk fell I watched from a respectable distance as the funeral rites were carried out. An old man, who I assumed to be a priest, was speaking. Tanvi saw I was watching and walked back to join me. In a whisper she interpreted the old man' words.
"He is saying the Spirit is neither born nor does it die at any time. It does not come into being or cease to exist. It is unborn, eternal and permanent. The Spirit is not destroyed when the body is destroyed."

I knew that the whole village believed this and I wished that I did too but at the time my western, analytical brain continued to doubt and question this belief that I was later to fully realise and accept.

Tanvi reached out and touched my arm.
"Thank you for what you have done for us today."
I looked around at the devastation and suffering and felt very humbled at her gratitude to me for having done so very little. These were a very special and gentle people.

The next morning Bandhu and I left early. As soon as we had earth underneath us that wasn't burnt I put Bandhu into a fast canter. I didn't know if I was running away from the horror behind me or avoiding the long and involved task of staying to help rebuild the village but I had come this far and I had to know what was in store for me, even though I felt guilty about leaving. I glanced back to see Tanvi watching me go. For a moment I hesitated and pulled back on the reins but then pushed Bandhu on.

The next stop was the Ganges and although Bandhu had proved his adeptness in water I didn't fancy the idea of swimming across a river known for its association with hepatitis, typhoid and cholera. That's of course if you lived that long to contract any such disease after escaping the crocodiles. So, we headed along the north bank looking for a dryer place to cross. After a few miles we came to one of India's many temples. This one was dedicated to the god Krishna, said to be the embodiment of love and divine joy and destroyer of all pain and sins. I had an unexplained desire to go into the temple; a strange feeling for me as I have never had an interest in any sort of religion whatsoever and in fact I had become a committed atheist after Charlie died. The Christian religion especially made me angry. God of love? Jesus loves all the little children? How could I believe in any such shit after helplessly watching my girl die in terrible pain for over a year? If reincarnation is real and Charlie's spirit still lives somewhere, I didn't believe it had anything to do with a god preached by clergy wearing dog collars and expensive ceremonial robes and worshipped by people who do so out of fear of an afterlife of hell and damnation if they didn't worship the Almighty. But despite my prejudice I was drawn to the temple. I felt a sort of energy, coming from inside that I had never experienced before. It was an overwhelming happiness that was being endured by whoever or whatever was in the temple.

I tied Bandhu to a tree outside and pushed open the heavy wooden doors. Except for an arrangement of flowers and what looked like some sort of memorial at the altar the temple was empty. But how could this be? Where was this incredible energy coming from? As I got closer to the altar I could see a framed photograph, among the flowers, of a young couple taken on what appeared to be their wedding day. They were dressed in colourful clothes and their hands were decorated with the same henna design.

As I looked at the picture I felt a presence behind me. I turned around to see a middle-aged woman approaching the altar. She carried fresh flowers, which she placed by the picture. She smiled at me and said, *"This is my son and his wife; they were married here. A week later both of them were drowned in a flood."*
"I'm so sorry for intruding and for your terrible loss."
"I like to tell people about them," she

continued. *"They were very much in love. Sweethearts since they were both twelve years old."*

I then realised what was happening to me. The energy that I was sensing was coming from them; it was still present in the temple. Even though they weren't there it was as powerful as if they still were and I could feel it. I wanted to tell the boy's mother but felt that I couldn't as I thought that, as a complete stranger, I didn't have the right to experience something so personal to her.

She continued to tell me her story.
"My name is Ragini, I am a doctor. I studied in America and worked in a hospital there for three years. I returned to India to continue to practice medicine, met my husband and we had our son – we called him Rudra, which means the remover of pain. I thought it was a perfect name for a doctor's son."

She smiled as she touched Rudra's face in the picture.
"He wanted to be a doctor too. So did his wife, her name was Ganika. They were due to travel to Europe only two days after they died. What is your name and what brings you here?"

I introduced myself but thought it was best if I was a little economical with the real reason I was in India as it was still somewhat weird to me let alone what she might think of my bizarre story. I told her that I had lost a child too and I had always wanted to visit India.

"Is that your horse outside?" she asked.
"Yes it is."
"So you decided to visit India on a horse?"
I told her that my daughter loved horses and it was in memory of her. I didn't want her to think that she had come across an English nutter in a place that meant so much to her.
"That's a lovely thing to do," she said.
"Would you like some refreshment and meet my husband?"
"That's very kind I'd like that."
I untied Bandhu and led him as we walked.
"Tell me about your daughter Tim."
"Her name was Charlotte but I always called her Charlie, she died of cancer," I answered.
"She wanted to study medicine as well…to become a vet."
Ragini smiled. *"She must have been very compassionate, and of course, intelligent."*
"Yes she was…life is cruel isn't it?"

Ragini nodded in agreement. She pointed to the Tilaka on my forehead.
"Someone must be very fond of you to give you that."
"Yes his name is Amar, a mystic – I stayed with him for a while."
Again I thought it best if I didn't tell the whole story."
"It will serve you well on your journey."
"Yes that's what he said," I answered.

We arrived at Ragini's house where I met her husband Hari, a colonel in the Indian Army. The house was a fabulous traditional building with a veranda surrounding a water garden. Soft classical Indian flute music was coming from speakers hidden in the plants, which endorsed the sound of water cascading from a central fountain. The refreshments that Ragini had promised turned into a lavish meal, which was a welcome break from the basic energy sustaining food that was packed into my saddlebag. There was even a selection of fresh raw vegetables for Bandhu who was given the freedom of a field at the back of the house.

We talked about our lost children, sharing fond memories and funny stories. Their son, like

Charlie, was an only child so there was an affinity with each other's anecdotes even though our children had lived miles and cultures apart. Each amusing recollection was equaled by the next storyteller until very soon all three of us were laughing uncontrollably. There was a pause in our laughter as we realised what we were doing; then Hari started to cry. He tried to stifle his emotion, which only caused all of us to start sobbing.
"I'm sorry," said Hari, "that's not the behaviour befitting a senior officer."
We looked at each other and started to laugh again…then continued crying.

Laughing and crying with someone all in the space of a couple of hours was certainly a short cut to what felt like a lifelong friendship. We carried on talking about our kids, owning up to regrets that each of us had ranging from not buying a toy that was begged for, to putting our careers first and not spending valuable time with them that couldn't be reclaimed. We even talked about the funerals right down to the masses of orange and white chrysanthemums that adorned the coffins of Ragini's and Hari's son and daughter in law and how I was amazed to discover how many

friends Charlie had that not only filled the crematorium but also the car park outside. Then Ragini asked a question that I wasn't expecting
"Do you believe in reincarnation?"
"I think I do but I also think that I've been deceiving you."
It was time to own up. I told them my story starting with my meetings with David and how Amar had been my mentor guiding me through the discoveries of my new insights. Before I told them about my experience of feeling the energy of their son and his bride in the temple I waited for their reaction, cautious that they may think I'm crazy and politely ask me to leave.

Hari was the first to comment. *"Amar is Hindu and we are Sikh but we have one thing in common...we all believe."*
Ragini carried on, *"we're not really religious people but what we have both witnessed leaves us in no doubt. I have seen patients, moments before death, experience something beyond logical explanation, as if they are being reborn."*

Hari nodded his head as he added, *"And I have*

seen men who have received mortal injuries in battle also display what seems to be a passing on to another life. The consistency is astounding."

I told them what I had felt outside the temple that had urged me to go in. they held hands as they listened intently.

"Thank you Tim," said Ragini. *"Can you teach me how to feel it too?"*

"I'm sorry Ragini I can't because I don't know how, but I know that I'm going to learn more and when I do I'll come back and see you again."

It was time to go. Hari told me where I could cross the river by ferry.

"You won't have to pay," said Ragini *"Not with that symbol on your head."*

"What does it actually mean?" I asked.

"It tells people, both Hindu and Sikh, that you are a student of a mystic on a journey of great importance. Even the poorest of people will do all that they can to help."

She was right the Tilaka was my fully paid-up ticket and I not only crossed the river for free but also enjoyed the hospitality of various people along the way from snacks, water and food for Bandhu to a bed for the night. In fact, sometimes the welcome and reaction was a bit OTT. One old woman gave me a splendid meal and when I had finished she appeared with a bowl of water and a towel and offered to bathe me. Not wanting to offend her hospitality I thought I'd better not refuse, thinking it was just going to be a hands and face ablution. It wasn't, in fact she was very thorough and gave me a complete valet and anointed me with very pleasant smelling oils after the extensive drying process. I'm still not sure whether it was an old custom or just an old woman having fun.

Unlike the first few days' feelings of uncertainty and trepidation I was now enjoying my journey through this wonderful country. Everyone I met was welcoming and gentle. Word would pass from one village to the next. People would come out of their homes to have a look and children would point and giggle at the strange Englishman on the black horse. I received invitations to weddings and birthdays to bring good luck and accepted them all as the food was always amazing.

One of these celebrations took place at a

beautiful spot called Dhuandhar Falls. The word Dhuandhar is derived from two Hindi words- Dhuan meaning smoke and Dhar denoting flow because mist created by water falling on the hard rocks below creates images of smoke billowing from the riverbed. This particular party that I was invited to bring good luck to was for a teenage boy's coming of age, birthday. A tent had been put up on the bank of the river and the usual abundance of food was laid out on lavishly decorated tables.

The birthday boy and a group of his friends were having a diving competition off a large rock into the river at the base of the falls. Young girls were sitting on the bank giving their preferred level of applause for each dive. The more extreme and complicated the dive, the louder and more enthusiastic the ovation. I noticed that someone else was watching the display from about fifty yards up the river. It was another boy of around the same age. I tied Bandhu to a bush and walked along the bank towards him. As I got closer I could see that his face was quite disfigured. It looked like a birth deformity rather than an accident. There was one thing that was very obvious - he wasn't a guest at the party. I didn't know whether it was his choice or if he wasn't invited. As I approached he tried to hide his face by looking away. I said hello and waited until he was ready to turn around. After a few seconds he turned half round still trying to hide his face and with no attempt at a smile.

I said hello again, this time in Hindi – one of the very few words I knew.
"Namaste"
He put his hands together, bowed his head and replied.
"Namaste."
As he gained a little more confidence he gave me a hint of a grin. Even though his face was so deformed I will always remember seeing how his eyes lit up and how I felt his energy change from fear to trust. I pointed to the boys upriver and asked, the best I could, using various hand gestures if he could dive. He nodded enthusiastically, leapt to his feet and shinnied up an overhanging tree. He stood for a second, arms outstretched then succeeded to perform a spectacular double somersault dive, entering the water with a splash no bigger than if a small bird had dived in to catch a fish. I clapped as loud as I could to attract the attention of the girls and boys at the party. It

got their attention, so I told the boy to do another dive. He shot back up the tree like a cat and did a dive even better than the first one. This time everyone was watching and after a moments pause of disbelief all of the girls stood up and applauded followed by the boys who jumped up and down splashing the water with their hands.

One of the girls beckoned the boy to come and join them. The rest of the girls backed up the invitation as did, one by one, the boys. The boy looked at me as if seeking approval.
"Go, go," I shouted urgently.
He ran towards the party, looking back at me a couple of times. When he got about twenty feet away he stopped. Shit, I thought, he isn't going to do it, but then one of the girls ran forward, grabbed his hand and walked along with him to join the group.
He called back to me, *"dhanyavaad."* (Thank you)

I never got to know his name and never needed to. I'll always remember him as 'The Boy'.

I glanced at the old compass and continued to head southwest enjoying the warmth and hospitality of so many wonderful people. Each town and village had a story to tell, a god to worship and a gift to stuff into my saddlebag. The countryside was a compendium of sights and sounds. Miles of flatland became days of mountains that eventually gave way to forests. Each vista had its own soundtrack from the high-pitched scream of eagles to the chattering of monkeys. Apprehension had all but left me except for the possibility of being attacked by a tiger, which never happened; in fact I never even saw or heard one. I was feeling confident and looking forward to what lay ahead at my destination, which was now only a few days away. But before that I was to face a sad and terrible tragedy.

We were coming down from a mountain and the usual sure-footed Bandhu was starting to stumble as if losing his concentration. I was picking up an energy that I can best describe as a flickering light bulb that was about to blow. I soon realised that it was Bandhu's energy that I was sensing. He kept on going but was finding it more and more difficult.

When we got to the bottom of the mountain he stopped. My legs felt wet with his sweat even though it wasn't particularly hot that day. He then started to tremble and his back legs started to cross over as if he was trying to feel the ground underneath him. A few seconds later he stood motionless and it was then that I heard him. It was as clear as if he was talking to me. He told me to get off him, as he was about to go down. I dismounted from his left side and as soon as my feet touched the ground he fell to his right so as not to hurt me. It was the last thing he ever did for me. I think he was dead before he hit the ground.

I stayed with Bandhu until a family of five appeared on a single motorbike. The Dad of the group said he thought that Bandhu had suffered a heart attack or maybe a stroke. He offered to get some men in his village to dispose of the body. I assumed Bandhu was going to supply the village with food for a few months. I didn't really want that to happen to my loyal companion but I knew it was the best option, so I agreed and thanked him.

I cut off a piece of Bandhu's mane, tied it in a bow and put it the saddlebag that I slung over my shoulder. I stood and stared for a while; first at Bandhu's lifeless body and then at the dirt road ahead.

I'd learnt so much about myself from being with Bandhu. Horses don't know how to be anything other than who and what they are. They can't hide their feelings like we can or pretend to know what they don't. Horses teach us that it's healthy to always be who we truly are.

They aren't concerned about the past or the future. They don't suffer from the stress that humans experience by dwelling on what has happened and what might happen. Horses are always in tune with the present moment so that they can keep themselves content and safe.

After facing danger they have the ability to return, almost immediately, to being calm. They don't worry about the next time a predator might appear or what they would have done differently the last time they encountered danger.

I used to think that I was an expert in communication but horses are true masters. If you feel tense, angry, or aggressive it's pointless telling them that everything is OK; they will only hear the truth through your body language. Everything that they do is by instinct, something that we have long since left behind in the jungles, forests and mountains where we used to live. I would like to think that Bandhu was an exceptional horse but maybe it was me who was short on loyalty, honesty and compassion and he was just a horse doing what came naturally to him. So much for his tiny brain compared to my huge one. I never got bored on my journey with Bandhu; it was a continual dialogue of senses. He would make me aware of something that he would hear, see or smell. The call of an animal, the movement caused by wind through the trees, the smell of something different that suddenly drifted through the air that caught his attention would be communicated to me by how he moved his body or altered his breathing. And I would respond by sending back signals with my body of how I felt about what he was telling me. The more relaxed I appeared the more reassured he became. We would gain our confidence from each other.

Now I was on my own, on foot to the finish line. Why? I still didn't have a clue. Turning back wasn't an attractive option as I was fourteen days into my journey and a mere four

days away from whatever was waiting for me at the Myanmar Gate. It may sound strange to say 'without someone to talk to' but as well as the silent conversations that Bandhu and I shared I also used to talk to him as if he was a human friend.
"Lovely day today Bandhu"
"Looks like rain ahead"
"Wow it's a hot one today boy"
"Let's stop for a while fella"
And other such spontaneous comments that seemed perfectly normal at the time.

Without my travelling companion to occupy me my head became full of whys and whats. Why did I decide to do this? Why am I becoming someone that I don't seem to know anymore? Why is there so much I don't know? What will I become? What other trials lie ahead? What if I don't achieve what Amar has planned for me? And most important of all – what the fuck am I doing walking along a dirt road in India heading for complete uncertainty with a vague hope of seeing and talking to Charlie the way I've been able to connect with a complete stranger called David when I should be in England trying to come to terms with my loss and get my life back on track?

After a day of walking in somewhat of a daze I came across a small village. An old couple welcomed me with food and a bed in their run-down farm out-building for the night. As I settled down amongst the straw and old sacks I looked up to see there was a hole in the roof that revealed a clear night sky of stars, giving me a backdrop to reflect on my experiences throughout my journey so far.

A few things that I hadn't considered up until then now seemed to have more meaning, and had relevance to Amar's words: *"The purpose of your journey is to gain faith in yourself and your ability to confront and prevail over obstacles beyond what you have experienced in the past."*

First there was the introduction to riding a horse. Not by having weeks of lessons in a fenced off riding school wearing a hard-hat and back protector vest but by believing I could do it; the same way I believed I could walk a tightrope.

Next there was the burnt-out village where everyone had lost faith after such a terrible disaster. Yet because I appeared to have been sent to help and then stepping forward to bury the child it was enough for the villagers to believe in themselves, confront the tragedy and start to rebuild their lives.

Then there was the encounter in the temple, which led to meeting Ragini and Hari. Just by telling them about the experience I had feeling the energy of their son and daughter in law I was able to give them some comfort and hope for the future and maybe even to enhance their belief in reincarnation and the possibility of being able to make some sort of contact with their son one day.

For me the most amazing experience was meeting 'The Boy'.

Cruelly disfigured by nature he had made his own decision to isolate himself from what he really wanted to be part of either because of the fear of being ridiculed by others or upsetting the other kids because of, what he thought, was his frightening appearance. But with encouragement he overcame everything that was holding him back and I was so touched by being able to play a part in his metamorphosis just by believing I could help to give him a better life. Whenever I thought of giving up during the weeks, months and years that followed and returning to a simpler life I would think of 'The Boy 'and what he had managed to overcome. He became my silent mentor.

I don't know whether it was because I felt good or I was just knackered from walking instead of riding but I slept like a log that night. I woke up feeling pretty good too, energised by realising what I had achieved so far and the fact that the Myanmar Gate at Igatpuri was only a day away.

I arrived at the Myanmar Gate as the sun was about to set, which must have been the best time to see it as the dusk light made the myriad of ornate carvings on the gate glow against the twilight sky. The gate was at least fifty feet high and looked like it should have been in Thailand rather than India. Four large round pillars encased an elaborate archway topped off by eight lavish gold tiers. At first I didn't notice the young man dressed in an ochre coloured Buddhist robe sitting on one of the stone benches. He caught my eye when he raised his hand to me.

"You must be Tim," he said as I approached him. *"Namaste"*

"Namaste" I said, putting my hands together and bowing my head to return his greeting. He smiled and took my saddlebag.

"Come with me please." I followed him away from the gate towards some distant hills. He looked to be in his mid-twenties, was clean-shaven, including his head. His skin, that looked like it had just been freshly made, was very pale and as smooth as bone china.

We arrived at a small, single storey building that looked like it was wedged between two hills. Thick wooden columns supported a sloping tiled roof. An ancient carved double door was open and the smell of incense was escaping into the evening air. The inside contained very little furniture and was dimly lit by a few candles. I could feel a very powerful energy in the room, which didn't seem to match the figure of a withered old man, dressed the same as the young man, sitting on a low couch. He raised his head in my direction and I assumed, from his closed eyes, that he was blind.

"Amar has told me all about you." He said.

How and when he had told him I hadn't a clue but I wasn't too surprised that they knew each other.
"How was your journey?"
"Eventful," I replied.
He smiled. *"Welcome to my home, it is yours for as long as you need it."*
To do what?" I asked
"To discover."
He was right; I discovered more than I ever could have imagined.

I didn't count the days I stayed there and I never got to know the inspiring old man's name, there was no need to really. He never mentioned mine so I never asked his. Those things didn't seem to matter compared with every new experience that did during my time there. I would go to bed every night exhausted from each new insight I had been become aware of and wake up every new day eager and excited to learn more.

From my first day with the old man it was clear that he was to Buddhism what Amar was to Hinduism; two visionary old men with a wealth of knowledge and awareness to impart…but why me? That's what I was still unsure of.

Having recently qualified as reaching middle age the last thing that I thought I would need to learn would be how to breathe but that was how I was to spend the first few days of my introduction to meditation. Amar had told me that this particular trial was to gain faith in myself but I was also beginning to learn who I was and what I was able to become. It's near on impossible for me to attempt to explain what those days with the old Buddhist did for me but a quote from The Buddha himself comes pretty close to defining it.

"The mind is everything. What you think you become. Meditation brings wisdom; lack of medition leaves ignorance. Know well what leads you forward and what holds you back and choose the path that leads to wisdom."

I was quite happy to stay at the house between two hills for as long as the old Buddhist would have had me but one morning I woke to find no one was there. I waited for a while before making my way back to the Myanmar Gate to see if the young man was where I had first met him. He wasn't but a familiar face was, it was

Vimal, sitting in a beaten-up old car with a rickety horse trailer attached to the back. Vimal looked around for Bandhu. I shook my head and put my hand on my heart. He gave me a sad look and understood that my travelling companion hadn't made the journey but didn't seem too concerned, obviously believing that Bandhu's spirit was now in another body.

I don't know what surprised me more – seeing Vimal a thousand miles from home or the thought of him being able, and allowed, to drive. I was soon to discover that his driving left a lot to be desired, especially the fact that he was unable to hear all of the honking from other drivers as he cut them up in his own silent, oblivious world. The journey back took a few days with brief stops for sleep and leg stretching. The lack of conversation didn't seem to be a problem; in fact there was a kind of exchange as every time I looked across at Vimal he would give me one of his warm and genuine smiles, which seemed to substitute for the absence of sound between us. He would also point to anything of interest along the way, which ranged from ornate temples to wild animals.

We arrived at the house and were greeted by Amar who listened intently to my adventures. As I told him about what I had learnt on my journey he seemed to be as pleased as I was. He smiled and said, *"It is not until faced with unforeseen adversity that we begin to understand how strong our spirit is. You believed in yourself and your ability even though you had no guarantee that you would survive. Your mind is beginning to open, and your spirit is prepared for what is to come."*

He didn't expand on what was to come despite me trying to probe but we did have a few hours of enjoyable conversation prior to me turning in for the night. Before climbing into bed I instinctively reached for the book. A new translation had been entered alongside the next page of Sanskrit.

You are braver than you believed, stronger than you imagined and wiser than you thought

As I closed my eyes and started to fall asleep I saw the faces of Tanvi, Ragini and Hari and 'The Boy' and hoped that through what I had experienced by meeting each of them they too had become braver, stronger and wiser.

Trial 3 – Mauna मौनम् (Silence)

Although I knew that my next trial was imminent Amar asked nothing of me for the following few weeks and I was in no hurry to find what was going to be asked of me. For the first time in years I didn't feel impatient, frustrated or in any way stressed. Every day I would spend hours developing my meditation technique. During each session, at the point when I had emptied my mind of anything useless to me, I would combine my clear state with the ability to feel whatever form of energy was close by. The result was much more powerful than I had experienced before. Even with closed eyes I was able to know whether an insect that had entered the room was a butterfly, wasp or mayfly. It was like being able to put every source of energy that I felt under a microscope. If nothing ever came of my time in India this would be one hell of a party trick to perform back in Taunton.

At first I found the experience a bit scary and quite overpowering but after a while I was able to control exactly when I wanted to choose to sense an energy rather than it always filling my head. The phenomenon was amazing. I would feel connected to whatever I tuned into, sharing whatever they were doing. I could even feel them breathing and their hearts beating.

The excitement was too much to contain. I wanted to tell Amar what I was experiencing and ask how I could use it to connect somehow with Charlie.

I told him that I felt like shouting what I had learnt to the world. He answered in his usual serene and controlled way.
"It appears that you are ready for your next trial."
I then bombarded Amar with questions; not allowing him time to respond to any of them before I fired off the next. They ranged from the obvious question of what is the next trial to what will I gain from it? When Amar answered I knew why he thought I was ready for my next trial.

"You are to encounter a period of Mauna, which is Sanskrit for silence."

This deservedly silenced my impulsive motormouth and I stood quietly as, after a brief pause, he explained further.

"Mauna means being intentionally silent, a discipline through which spiritual experiences will arise. It doesn't just mean not speaking but total silence - silence of the mind, to gain an increased receptivity towards sound. Subsequently, like the still water of a lake that reflects things as they are, the calming effect of silence helps us to see things more clearly and therefore be in a deeper connection with ourselves and those around us. Total silence is not speaking to anyone or anything including yourself whether out loud or in thought. You mustn't partake in any form of communication like writing and reading. Silence of the mouth is merely the beginning of Mauna. In time you will learn to silence your mind in order to gain a greater perception for you to communicate on a higher level than you are currently able. Only when the mind is pure and calm, will you be able to 'see' the truth of everything as it

really is and not be contaminated by the impurities and restlessness of the mind."

I first thought that not talking would be easy; after all, apart from Amar who was there to talk to? The most difficult thing was going to be if I happened to bang my head or stub my toe and not be able to shout, *"fuck it"* or *"bollocks."* But the difficulties that I was to discover were not being able to have mental conversations with myself as everyone does instinctively and constantly. Or not saying hello to a bird that happens to attract my attention when I was in the garden. Silence of the mind was so hard for the first week of silence and Amar said I was to practice it for six weeks to even start to experience the benefit of Mauna. I began to get bad headaches by desperately trying to not think of anything but that only resulted in trying to think of not thinking and the more I tried the more vicious circles I invented for myself.

The other thing that would make me feel angry with myself was I always had a song in my head. No song in particular just any old song that I would wake up singing to myself and couldn't shake off. The more I tried the worse it became. The most ironic song that filled my head one morning was 'The sound of silence' by Simon and Garfunkel, and how the hell was I supposed to stop thinking of Charlie – the reason I was doing all this? The more I emptied my head the more she filled it.

Then it dawned on me. This was what I was really like - continually talking whether out loud or in thought. When I realised this, Mauna became easier. For the first time in my life I was able to listen without arguing or commenting. I didn't have to waste time inwardly talking to myself about things that didn't matter. I could just look, listen and learn. I didn't need to have an opinion about what was around me. I learnt that listening was not just what your ears could do but what all your senses were capable of receiving when your mind is clear of your own thoughts. I could listen with my eyes, my nose and even taste what I was listening to. Everything was more intense. I became aware of the intricacies of what I used to either not even notice or care about.

This became apparent one late afternoon while sitting in the garden. I was listening to what the outside world was telling me without commenting or even thinking. The usual, individual jungle sounds were vying for attention against their competitors. Chattering monkeys were trying to outdo the parrots, chirping cicadas were attempting to drown the sound of singing crickets and the sound of the early evening breeze through the trees was filling in every brief silence in between. A young deer emerged from the undergrowth and lowered its head towards a patch of lush grass. I focused my attention on the deer and managed to block out everything else. Although I was about fifteen feet away from it, I could hear her breathing softly and rapidly as if her face was pressed against mine. I could smell the freshness of the grass that she was smelling; so intense, it was as if my nose was an inch away from the earth.

And then the ultimate sensation happened. I could taste the grass that she started to eat. Although there was nothing in my mouth I could actually taste what she was eating. I heard the deer swallow as my own throat did the same. Tears ran down my face as I spontaneously expressed my excitement at this new experience. Could it be possible that I could now hear, even when my ears could hear no sound? Had I grown another sense? Was this what David meant by 'The inner sight'? These questions that I was asking myself and were filling my head had broken my silence which annoyed me as I was only into my fourth week and I had two more weeks to go of remaining silent. I decided to take stricter measures to ensure my silence so I would stab myself in the arm with a knife, that I got from the kitchen, every time I succumbed to having silent conversations with myself. I never thought that I would ever resort to middle-age self-harm, but the idea seemed to work and I was soon silent and observing where I had left off after the ear and eye opening encounter with the deer.

I wanted to experience more so I would sit for hours clearing my mind to be able to hear what the world was saying. It could be a bird having a conversation with another distant bird and like the deer I would hear, smell and taste what it was doing. The more I was able to control my own silence the more I heard. Each animal, not only had its own language it had its own perceptions, motives and fears. I would hear a sparrow sense when there was a hawk nearby and hear a lizard's breathing become shallow when it was about to catch a fly, but I wanted to hear another human's silent thoughts. Amar had left to go on one of his mysterious journeys, so I homed in on Vimal.

At first I didn't know if it was going to be possible as this was someone who, not by his own choice, had been silent all his life. There was no way that there would be a song in his head because he had never heard music, but I discovered that Vimal's world of silence was far from quiet.

Contrary to Vimal's lack of hearing his other four senses that were in working order were supercharged. To him it must have been normal but to me it was mind-blowingly deafening. The vibration that I could feel he was feeling through his fingers as he chopped some herbs was like a Buddy Rich drum solo played at volume ten. The smell as the knife blade cut through the herbs was as potent as squirting a concentrated mixture of the herbal pulp up both of my nostrils and as he licked a tiny piece of coriander off his finger the taste exploded in my mouth. He glanced out of the window at a distant hawk that was hovering in search of its prey and, through his eyes, I could see every individual feather of the hawk as if I was holding it in my hand. Borrowing Vimal's remaining senses for that short time was an intoxicating experience. This wasn't just someone who had four highly developed senses this was a beautiful species of human being that was different to me.

The more I listened to Vimal the more I wanted to hear. I never sensed any anger, frustration or sadness about his inability to hear and talk. He was grateful for the life that he had and sincere in everything that he did. Being able to just listen to him was very humbling. He would see what most people never saw and enjoy an intensity of feeling far beyond normal human perception. His name, meaning pure, was the perfect dictionary definition, relating to sound, that defined his personality: perfectly in tune and with a clear tone.

My appreciation of Mauna hit its real peak a few weeks later when I was sitting in my room. After quite a long period of time I had managed to achieve an intense state of calm and was completely separated from trivial thoughts. It was like floating around in whatever space I chose to be in. Then something interrupted the tranquility. It was like a cry for help coming from somewhere in the forest. Not an audible sound, more like a sense similar to what I had experienced listening to the deer and Vimal. But this was different. It was very faint and I wasn't totally sure whether I was hearing, or should I say feeling, anything at all. At first I tried to ignore it but after a short while I couldn't. Whatever it was, it was desperate and frightened.

I followed my instinct out into the garden and then into the jungle. It was though I had a built-in sat nav guiding me to whatever was obviously distressed. I walked for about twenty minutes through the dense jungle until I came across a small clearing. Sitting on a fallen tree was a small child crying. She was clearly lost and kept calling out.
"Mamma, Mamma"
I didn't need a translator to know what she was saying.
I approached her slowly and held out my hand. She looked away and called out louder.

"Mamma"
I called on my very limited command of Hindi to say hello
"Namaste"
Luckily another word I knew in Hindi as well as hello was friend.
"Mitr" I said, pointing at myself.
The little girl looked at me. She must have only been around four years old. Eventually she took my hand as I led her back to Amar's house.
"We find Mamma," I said hoping she would understand.

Amar recognised the girl and we set off in the mule cart to the village where she lived. A very distraught young woman, who was obviously Mamma, greeted us through tears of joy at seeing that a tiger hadn't eaten her daughter after all. She hugged the little girl as Amar told her where I had found her. The woman grabbed my hands and kissed them repeatedly. This marked a very happy ending to my introduction to Mauna.

That night I couldn't help thinking that when David had saved Charlie from drowning had he heard her cry for help the same way that I had heard the little girl lost in the jungle? I reached for the Sanskrit book and read the next handwritten translation.

The quieter you become the more you will be able to hear. Through the doors of silence, the light of wisdom and peace will shine upon you.

The night had become very cold. I pulled the blanket up close to my face and thought I could hear snow falling.

Trial 4 –Solitude

Winter had arrived – I woke very early the next morning to see the garden had a very slight dusting of snow, which was virtually unheard of in that part of the country. This sort of weather only happened further north. Vimal was in a state of childlike excitement, pointing to the sky to express his fascination of the bizarre weather that he had never seen before. Amar was smiling at the boy's enjoyment of the freak manifestation. Within an hour, as the temperature quickly reached fifteen degrees centigrade, the snow had all gone and very soon the garden returned to a pleasant twenty three degrees, like a perfect English summer.

Amar had told me to take time to practice and develop what I had learnt and to let him know when I thought I was ready to continue with my studies.

Weeks and months went by and I had no desire to return to England, especially knowing that I still l had a lot to learn about myself. Being in India was the only place where I was going to discover the person I was to become. This felt like my home despite some of the hardships of the trials that I had endured so far. I had realised that falling in love isn't restricted to a person. I was completely in love with India.

One afternoon after a period of deep meditation I told Amar that I was ready.

He led me out into to the garden, sat down beside me and summed up my next trial in a single sentence:
"The artist Picasso said, without great solitude, no serious work is possible."
"I'm no match for Picasso," I said, *"but I'm willing to try a little solitude if you think I'll achieve some serious work. I hope I won't feel too lonely"*

Amar gave me one of his familiar serious looks.

"Real solitude is a state of being alone without being lonely and will lead to great self-awareness and discovery. It will bring peacefulness and a state of inner richness. From solitude you will draw sustenance. You have reached a point in your journey when you must be alone to refresh yourself. Use all that you have discovered so far. Sense what is around you, believe in yourself and have credence in your ability to go further and listen without comment or argument. Combine everything that you have achieved so far and you will find your next reward that will bring you closer to the inner sight."

So, I was to become a hermit, which didn't really bother me; in fact I was quite looking forward to solitude. I'd been a fan of the writer Thomas Mann for years and loved his quote, *"Solitude gives birth to the original in us, to beauty unfamiliar and perilous – to poetry. But also, it gives birth to the opposite: to the perverse, the illicit, the absurd."*

But even though I'd got used to being and traveling on my own I had also got used to Vimal always being there and the occasional appearance of Amar. Even when I was alone with Bandhu I was never actually alone. As well as him to talk to there were always people to meet along the way.

"How long am I to be in solitude?" I probed.
"It will take time." Answered Amar.
"A week, two weeks, six?" I continued.

"The fact that time still seems to be your master suggests that this trial is what you really need to do. Giving yourself the pressure of time will only restrict you from gaining a high level of awareness and understanding. The solitude that you need to experience is to be one year."

"A year?" I shouted.

"By questioning the time you need you are either doubting your ability to achieve what I have told you or you have something else that you think you need to do. You must learn to live your life at the speed of nature. A flower knows when the time is right to grow from the

earth. If it were to rush it would die. You must stop being a servant of the clock."

As usual, Amar was right. I put my hands together, bowed my head and apologised for raising my voice.

"No need to apologise Tim – we will leave tomorrow."
I thought it best not to ask where I was going to spend my solitude as my questions were beginning to sound banal to say the least and like the previous trials, I was sure to find out.

The next morning Amar was harnessing the old mule to the cart that contained a goat and not much else. Hardly what you would call adequate supplies for the year ahead I thought. The only things I took were my razor and soap, as I didn't want to look like a mad bearded hermit if I was to meet anybody, and a change of clothes supplied by Vimal. We headed west along a rough dirt road for about ten miles and then went south for another ten or so miles until we reached a spot by a narrow, fast flowing river.

"Your new home," announced Amar pointing

to a small, single storey building made from mostly mud with a straw roof. Next to it was an old wooden corral, which I assumed was for my only neighbour, the goat. Amar unloaded the goat into the corral and led me to the back of the house where there was a vegetable garden of sorts.

"Everything you need is here," said Amar. *"And there is plenty of fish in the river."*

He gave me a half round glass magnifying lens about the size of my hand.

"This is for lighting your fire."

He climbed back on the cart, bade me farewell and left.

The moment I walked into the house I could feel something. It was like the sensation that I felt in the temple where I sensed the energy of Ragini's son and daughter in law. It was familiar to me but at first I couldn't put my finger on it. It would come and go as I moved around the room, sat in a different place or stepped through the doorway. It started to piss me off that I couldn't place what I was sensing but something was certainly there and it was something that I was to discover more about later.

The first couple of days didn't feel much like solitude, as I was too busy exploring my new home, the surrounding area and thinking how best to survive. After a few attempts I finally managed to master milking the goat without her running off or trying to head-butt me. Nanny seemed a good enough name for her so that's what she became. Most of what I pulled up in the veg garden was recognisable and what wasn't familiar tasted pretty good anyway. I soon got to love the river. It was my source of fresh fish, my morning bath and a little further downstream, away from where I collected my drinking water, my bidet.

The simple pleasure of sitting in the fast-flowing water naked and having a shave was something I looked forward to every day – so much so that on the fourth day I decided to shave my head for practical and hygienic reasons. The effect it had on me was quite remarkable. I felt super cleansed, strangely pure and about ten years younger. I think the shaved head was what encouraged me to embark on a fitness regime, so every morning after my river ablutions I would go for a run then do a few aerobics before meditating.

I soon lost track of the days that went by but after about two weeks solitude started to kick in. After my daily routine and whatever chores I thought I needed to do like tending to the garden and gathering wood for the fire the rest of the days were for me to decide how best to spend the time that seemed to get longer each day.

One day I decided to think only of Charlie; to try and recapture every memory that I had with her, from holding her as a tiny helpless baby to trying to be as cool as her when she became a teenager. What I didn't realise was exactly how life changing this decision was going to be for me. The more I thought about each precious moment the more vivid it became, as if I was back in time. My new heightened senses combined with complete solitude seemed to amplify each memory. Every conversation I remembered was like hearing her voice again but somehow clearer and more intense than when it actually happened.

Even remembering pushing her on a swing in the park I could feel the warmth of her back. And carrying her around as a tiny tot when she was too tired to walk, I could hear her breath in my ear, smell her hair and feel her young skin against my cheek.

At first I thought that I would find this task too difficult and upsetting. Whenever I used to think of her before tears would fill my eyes and the thought of her not being there was unbearable. Soon after Charlie's death a bereavement counsellor said to me, *"losing a child is something that you never get over; you just find a more comfortable place to put the pain."* But now it was different. I was able to cherish every single moment of her life and play back precious times with her. I would even smile when I remembered some of the times that we used to laugh together.

During her last few days I so wanted to say sorry for not always being around as much as I could have been throughout her life but I knew that would have been like telling her she was dying.

The incredibly vivid memory that really did get to me was when I recalled sitting next to her three months before she died. A blanket was wrapped around her painfully thin body. She was very weak and unable to eat hardly anything. I made her some soup, which she managed to eat about three spoonfuls of and less than half a slice of bread. She smiled at me pleased that she had managed the meager portion. I smiled back, kissed her on the forehead and made an excuse to go to the bathroom where I burst into tears. It was one of the last and most overwhelming memories of my little girl, made even more powerful by my new, heightened senses. But even this memory meant that I could be with her again and look after her.

So now I could not only vividly recall my memories with Charlie, but I could also relive them whenever I chose to. I could hear her, touch her, smell her and even watch her play. This was like having the best dream possible, to be able to be virtually with her again whenever I wanted to even though she couldn't answer me I could talk to her. This put solitude in a totally different light, as I was now never alone and certainly not lonely. The only thing that I obviously couldn't do was collect and playback any new memories.

As the weeks went by I became more accomplished at combining silence with solitude, which may sound a bit crazy, as there was no one to talk to anyway but being so secluded enabled me to reach a much deeper sensation of silence faster than I'd ever experienced before. It was like being able to flick a switch and be in a different state of consciousness without very much effort of concentration, ready to home in on whatever I wanted to listen to intensely. From the house I could switch from hearing what a distant animal was experiencing to the wind blowing through bulrushes by the river, which was about two hundred yards away from the house.

One afternoon I was lying in a makeshift hammock that I'd rigged up on the small veranda of the house when I heard what could be best described as an assault on silence. At the time I was listening to a butterfly's wings disturbing the warm air around its body, making a sound like high-pitched baby sneezes.

Then suddenly all I could hear was a loud racket coming from the jungle, which I had to investigate. At first my heightened sense of sound thought it was something mechanical that was ripping the jungle apart but as I got closer it sounded more like some sort of battle taking place. It was coming from way above my head and was getting louder as I got nearer to it. The aggression was quite frightening but I had to know what it was, so I approached with some trepidation, looking up, as I got closer. Then all was revealed. A bear was attacking a bee's nest, hitting it and knocking segments of the honeycomb to the jungle floor whilst scooping up and eating the honey with its huge clawed paw. Even though the bear was the aggressor I could feel a sense of calm that he or she had, compared with the panic and desperation of every single bee that was desperately defending its nest. Although I thought it would be nice to gather up some of the honey for myself I decided it was best not to nick the predator's well-earned supper, as I didn't fancy the idea of a bear with a sore head tracking me back to the house.

On the way back to the house I started to feel very tired. It wasn't because I'd done anything exhausting to feel that way but I think it was due to me coming into close contact with another living thing after being on my own for so long that seemed to sap my energy. The contrast was draining. I remembered when I was filming a TV commercial in Montana years ago. Tahe film crew, of about twenty people, and me were miles from any town. The owner of the land where we were filming lived on his own in a small shack with only the company of a few animals. As a gesture of goodwill we invited him to have lunch with us. Because he turned out to be so charming and humble we invited him to join us again for breakfast the following morning but he didn't turn up, so we sent someone to his house to see if he was ok .We discovered that although he had really enjoyed the previous day he also found it very tiring being around so many people and felt that he couldn't take up the offer of breakfast as he was still feeling shattered. It was something that I found incredible at the time but as I sat down on a wooden bench on the veranda of the house I totally understood how he must have felt.

Maybe it was because I was tired and my head was completely empty of any thought, even that of Charlie, that I sensed, whatever it was, at the house, but this time it was much stronger. I didn't try and concentrate on working out what it could be – I just let it

happen, until I could feel a presence next to me. Then I heard a familiar voice.
"Hello Tim."
I opened my eyes. The first thing I saw was the two odd socks of David.
"Hello David," I said calmly. *"This is ridiculous."*
"It's only ridiculous if it isn't possible," said David, "and as anything is possible nothing is ridiculous."
"You know, I'm not sure whether it's Amar or you who's the master of the smart-arse comment," I replied.
David's laugh was so realistic I could have believed he was actually alive.
"So, it was your energy that I sensed on my first day here." I said, rather pleased with myself.

"No," answered David, *"It was my grandmother's, which is why you thought it was familiar to you. When my mother Priya left for England with my father, my grandmother moved to this house. When she died she left it to Amar who lived here for a long time. He still stays here from time to time to be with my grandmother who he loved*

dearly even though she refused to see him after my mother was born for the rest of her life."

I told David how I could now replay my memories of Charlie's life with amazing realism that gave me such a good feeling.
"Is this what Amar experiences when he's here?" I asked.
"Yes, and a lot more," David answered, *"They are completely together. You see despite my grandmother vowing never to see Amar after their love affair was discovered she truly loved him and after she died she was released from the conventions of guilt and free to love again. Because it is still such a powerful love they can now be together in their unrestricted out of body state."*
"What was, or should I say is, her name?" I asked.
"Sushma, which means a beautiful woman," answered David.

We spoke well into the night about everything that had happened to me. I didn't think it was at all strange that I was talking to someone who wasn't really there but if anyone had been watching they would have seen a crazy man with a shaved head talking to himself. I never thought of David as a ghost. There was no clichéd glow around him and no coldness in the air when he appeared like ghosts are supposed to be associated with. In fact, he was quite the opposite – very real with an enormous feeling of warmth.

I told David that I thought my life was now beginning to have a purpose. As I spoke about the burnt-out village and how I helped the people to rise above their tragedy, the hope I gave to Ragini and Hari about the death of their son, 'The Boy' whose isolated life changed despite his disfigured face and how I found the lost little girl, I started to cry with joy. David smiled and said, *"This is only the beginning Tim. Just the start of what you are to achieve."*

He had just one more thing to say before he left me to continue my solitude. *"We determine who we are by what we do."*

As the months went by I stopped counting how many days my solitude had lasted. It became less of a quest to see if I could endure it and more of an all-involving discovery of awareness. Not just an awareness of what was around me but a heightened self-awareness. The days became shorter as I meditated for what I thought were minutes but were in fact hours at a time. I would wake way before dawn, eager to discover more. I had become hooked on enlightenment to such an extent that something had to give and give it did. I had become blasé about having out of body experiences, the feeling of looking at myself whilst being in a state of almost hypnotic meditation had become like a routine. I was desperate to get to the next stage, whatever that was, so one morning I put myself in a trance like state and called upon all of my heightened senses at the same time with the intention of being taken there. It was then that all hell broke loose.

The German philosopher Friedrich Nietzsche said, *"Out of chaos comes order,"* and I was experiencing the first half of his quote… chaos. Everything seemed to be massively exaggerated. Every sound was ten times louder than it should have been. Everything I touched felt larger than it should have felt and my head was counting down to exploding. It was if I was experiencing every possible sense all at once and at volume ten. If I was to put a soundtrack to what I was experiencing it would have been composed by Philip Glass, something along the lines of his music from the film Koyaanisqatsi – a Native American Hopi word meaning 'Life out of balance.'

I knew I was staggering round the room but didn't have any idea where I was going. I must have blacked out because the next thing I remember I was outside by the river. As my eyes slowly opened chaos gave way to order and I knew that I had arrived at the next stage of my journey.

I felt exhausted but detoxed of any impurity and completely elated. When the tiredness subsided my mind felt sharp and more perceptive than I had ever experienced before. Even though my senses had already developed during my previous trials everything was now even more pronounced; colours were brighter, sounds were clearer, and I could even taste the air that I was slowly breathing. I felt alert and, not because of any religious reason, reborn. After a few more hours of getting used to this new awareness something else happened.

I was sitting outside the house and felt as if I was being told to cross the river urgently. It wasn't an energy or a sound that I was sensing like before, it was just a compulsion to get to the other side, like a magnet pulling me across that I couldn't ignore. I waded as far as I could and swam the rest. As I got closer to the other bank I could see movement behind some bushes. Thinking it was an animal that was either in distress or could eat me I approached cautiously.

Self-preservation instantly disappeared when I saw what I was facing.

A man, who looked to be in his fifties, was raping a teenage girl who had a gag tied tightly around her mouth to stop her screaming. The look in her eyes was complete terror. She saw me but the man didn't. As well as feeling her fear and pain I could also sense her extreme humiliation. It was as though she didn't want to be discovered and saved from her terrible ordeal. She closed her eyes forcing a torrent of tears to run down her face. I let out a spontaneous shout.
"No!"

The man looked up, startled and obviously scared. He quickly ran off, clumsily pulling up his pants as he made his escape. My instinct was to run after him and smash his head in with the nearest rock I could find but concern for the girl pulled me back. As I turned to help her, she ran off in the opposite direction. I called out but she kept on running. I could hear her sobbing long after she was out of sight. On the flattened area of grass where the terrible crime had taken place there were evidential drops of blood. I began to tremble with rage and had to sit down on the riverbank to stop my legs from giving way.

Back at the house I tried to make sense of what had just happened. How did I know that I had to go to the girl without sensing any energy that was being generated by her or that evil man? Was this another gift, to add to my newly acquired advanced senses, that had been bestowed on me, and if so by whom or by what? Or was it just a one-off? I tried to play back exactly what I felt at the time that I first knew that I had to cross the river but just felt irritated that I couldn't recapture the emotion that I had experienced. All I was able to realise was that nothing on earth would have been able to stop me. I should have felt privileged that I was able to intervene at such a crucial moment but I didn't. Instead, I was scared at the thought of becoming a different person, so much so that schizophrenia crossed my mind. I desperately wanted to know the symptoms and felt frustrated at not being able to Google it. But even if I could reassure myself that I didn't have a split personality, I still wouldn't know exactly what was really happening to me.

I wished I could talk to Amar who always had all the answers, or even David. I tried to concentrate in a futile attempt to summon him but it didn't work. Meetings were obviously on his terms and he didn't feel the need to turn up. This made me feel angry at the thought of being used for a purpose, which was obviously beyond both my control and my state of mind. I wanted to check whether I was still able to sense the energy of living things or had I lost that ability? I closed my eyes and listened to what the world was telling me. Everything was still in working order. I could sense distant movements of animals going about their hunting, mating and travels. I came to the conclusion that the plight of the young girl that

I sensed was so strong that it temporarily cancelled out anything else that I would normally have felt or heard. I just didn't have any other explanation for what I had just experienced. I resigned myself to the fact that I would never see the girl again or learn what happened to her but that proved to be quite the opposite.

Two days later I was out gathering wood for the fire. I sensed that there was an energy source close to the house, which was about a quarter of a mile from where I was. It felt to be about the size of a large animal or a small person. I made my way back as quickly and quietly as I could. As I got closer I saw the young girl running away from the house carrying something. I called after her but she disappeared into the jungle. My first thought was, surely she hadn't come to rob me and if she had she would have been very disappointed at the lack of anything of any value in the house. But I couldn't have been more wrong. On the table was a large bowl of, what I was later to discover was called Allahabadi Tehri, a delicious rice, masala and vegetable dish. Although my cooking skills had improved over the past months they were nowhere near as good as what I was about to enjoy. I felt touched by the girl's thoughtfulness and a little guilty of thinking she was a thief.

Later that same day I was due to go to the river to wash my one and only change of clothes that I knew I'd left on the floor near my bed, but they weren't there. So that's what she was running off with, but why did she want my dirty kurta and pants? I found out the next morning when I found them outside the door, washed, neatly folded and a beautifully mended tear in the pants.

That wasn't the only visit I had from the girl. I had regular meals and laundry delivered but she remained elusive and that bothered me. Maybe she was ashamed of the terrible ordeal she was experiencing when I rescued her. It would have been easy to catch her as most of the time I knew when she paid me a visit, but I didn't want to frighten her, so I made a plan to communicate with her from a distance. I started by leaving her some flowers next to the cooking pot or by my laundry. After a few more visits I put my old graphic design skills to the test. On a piece of wood I drew two faces in profile facing each other. The next day I drew in speech bubbles above their heads as if they were talking to each other.

It worked; the next day I was sitting outside and sensed her approaching. Rather than hide so she could make her delivery and leave, I waited where she could see me. Slowly she emerged from the jungle walking towards me very slowly, occasionally stopping to gain her confidence. I didn't get up to meet her I just sat and waited. When she was standing a few yards in front of me was the first time that I got a good look at her. To say she was skinny would have been an understatement, but despite the ragged clothes and tangled hair there was a natural beauty about her. Her eyes were large and alert. Her jaw was small with quite a pointed chin and even though her mouth looked a little too large for her face it gave her a distinctive look of all eyes and mouth. I pointed to myself and said, *"Tim."* She pointed to herself and said, *"Ladki."* My solitude had come to an end.

Over the next few days we spend time together swapping words of each other's language until we could almost hold a conversation. At first

Ladki was both nervous and cautious, which I put down to her being with a man similar in age to the one that had raped her but I was careful not to invade her space, never sitting beside her or getting too close. Ironically Ladki was about the same age as Charlie just before she had died and there were times when I would have loved to give her a fatherly hug but that would been both crazy and selfish. Day by day her subservience towards me changed to confidence and eventually we would sit side by side on the bench outside pointing to things we could see and telling each other what they were in our own language. I loved it when she would laugh at my pronunciation, which I would often get wrong on purpose just to hear her laughter. Ladki made me as happy as I could have been relative to losing Charlie and I looked forward to her visits and the food she brought that we were soon sharing.

I was also to discover that Ladki had a surprise in store for me. One day she turned up with a roll of paper that she laid out on the floor revealing a selection of drawings. There were people, animals, landscapes and some beautiful abstract designs. I pointed to her then the drawings, clumsily asking if they were hers. She nodded proudly. Her work was incredible. She wasn't just talented she was bordering on genius. Back in England any art gallery, design company or advertising agency would be fighting over her. I loved the fact that she was completely oblivious to this. After spending over twenty years in the design and commercial art business I felt quite humbled by both her perception and innocence.

I took one of the drawings and turned it over to the blank side of the paper and mimed drawing as I pointed to both of us with my other hand. *"We draw together, you and me we draw?"* She nodded enthusiastically and ran off into the jungle. I didn't know where her house or village was or whether she lived on her own or with her parents. I decided that if she wanted me to know she would have invited me. After a while she returned with paper, sticks of charcoal and even more enthusiasm than when she ran off.

During the following days and weeks we would draw together for hours and although there was never a word spoken I felt like there was a continuous dialogue between us. I hadn't drawn since art college due to being seduced by technology and the speed in which a computer can produce an image completely lacking in emotion that didn't seem to bother the commercial world that I was a fully paid up member of. The first time we drew together I dived straight in, scribbling away with my stick of charcoal trying to replicate a wild orchid that was our subject. I glanced away at Ladki and noticed that she wasn't drawing but just looking, which seemed to go on for about fifteen minutes. I watched her as she smiled at the flower. Her eyes were tracing its every form. She moved her head in synchronisation to the orchid's small movement from a sudden gentle breeze. She moved her hands in front of her face as if caressing the petals and then stopped and stared without a single blink. For a moment I thought that she had even stopped breathing. Without taking her eyes off the flower she reached for a stick of charcoal and with incredible speed expressed what she had seen. What she did took my breath away. There was I gifted with a heightened awareness, able to hear the wings of a distant butterfly and sense the energy of a deer hidden from view and here was a teenage girl with a visual awareness able to create something that looked more orchid-like than an orchid. Who taught her how to do this? I knew why I was now able to sense and hear what I once would have never thought possible. It was because of David and Amar and what they had exposed me to but where did she get it from? Taught by a famous artist or descended from one maybe? Surely it had to have come from somewhere.

As well as the obvious language restrictions I didn't want to ask her too many questions in case she had secrets that she didn't want to reveal. I didn't want to frighten her off and lose her company. What I knew about her was enough. She never tried to ask me what I was doing there, she just accepted that I was, and I felt the same about her. I did however want to protect and look after her in a Dad type of way. Sometimes when she was drawing I would look at her and wonder how anyone could abuse such innocence and purity, which would make me regret not killing the bastard who assaulted her.

All Dads love to show off to their kids so one day as we were drawing in a small clearing in the jungle something happened that enabled me to do just that. I sensed a distant energy that I had experienced before. It was a wild boar that I had sensed and seen on a couple of previous occasions and it was coming our way. I started to draw the boar from memory and tapped Ladki on the shoulder to show her my drawing. She was a little puzzled and looked around to try and see where the boar was that I had drawn. As I pointed to the jungle Ladki's jaw dropped open in amazement as the boar appeared right on cue.

With a wide-eyed, confused look on her face she said, *"Aapane aisa kaise kiya?"* (How did you do that?)
I put my finger on my forehead and said, *"third eye."*
Ladki laughed and gestured me to sit still as she started sketching my portrait. When she turned the drawing round to show me I saw she had drawn a stunning picture of me with a third eye.
Bhagwan Shiv," she said with a smile, who was the Hindu god with a third eye. That drawing has become one of my most treasured possessions.

I knew the end of my solitude was soon approaching although, because of Ladki's appearance, I had only done about nine months of the yearlong trial that Amar had set me. I could have quite happily stayed there for as long as Ladki was prepared to visit, which I knew couldn't last forever. She was a young girl with a future and a life to live. I tried to tell her about Amar and how he would turn up one day but we hadn't reached that level of understanding with the language difference and as much as I tried I could see the look of confusion on her face so I gave up and we just carried on drawing and laughing. I was enjoying my life that I thought just couldn't get any better as we shared our gifts of awareness. I learnt how to see what she could see and in return I would teach her how to listen to the world around us, which she would get very excited about. It made me wonder how many of the thousands of people that we brush past in the supermarket or sit next to on a train that we don't even notice but may just learn something incredibly rewarding from them if only we are prepared to communicate rather than be seduced by our blinkered, self-inflicted schedules.

One afternoon, as Ladki and I were sitting outside about to have our meal, I sensed a very familiar energy approaching. I could also hear the creaking of the wooden frame of Amar's mule cart long before it came into view. Although I would be pleased to see him I knew my life was about to change yet again. Of course I could have told Amar that I had found the life that I wanted but I felt I had a duty to perform even though I didn't know exactly what it was. My first thought was to put Ladki at ease. When the cart came into view I pointed at it and said *"Amar, mitr,* friend." She looked a little apprehensive but walked with me as I approached Amar.

Ladki and Amar greeted each other with the usual hands together and head bow as I introduced them to each other. I quickly told Amar the story of how we had met. He listened intently and sympathetically but looked a little confused at Ladki's name. *"No one is called Ladki,"* said Amar, *"it simply means girl. Let me speak to her."*

Amar spoke to Ladki in Hindi. They walked to the bench outside the house to carry on their conversation. I could still hear what they were saying but didn't know what it all meant. The energy I was sensing was incredibly warm with no hint of mistrust or suspicion from either of them. After a few minutes Amar put his hand on Ladki's head like a priest blessing her before walking back to me to reveal what he had discovered.

"First of all Tim let me congratulate you on your choice of friends. As well as a brave young girl she is honest and inspiring and she has a story that she wants you to know. Her mother was also raped and took her own life when your friend was a baby. The village that she came from brought her up but didn't treat her well as she was the result of a rape. They didn't even give her a name but instead called her Ladki, the girl, and made her do the sort of chores that were hard and dirty that no one else wanted to do. She left the village to live in a cave not far from here when she was about fourteen. She doesn't know exactly what age she was and still doesn't. After she leaves here she works for a few hours as a cook in the evenings in another small village. They pay her in essentials and paper for her drawings"

My eyes started to sting as I held back the tears. What sort of life had she lived as well as what I had witnessed the day I found her? The thought of her mother's history repeating itself must have been devastating for her and the fact that she didn't even have a real name was heartbreaking.

Amar paused for a second to allow me to take it all in before continuing.

"The day that you found her she was gathering herbs when a passing aavaara, what you would call a tramp, raped her. It appears that you turned up at the crucial moment before she became in danger of falling pregnant.

There is something that she wants you to know…you are the only friend she has ever had and she would like you to give her a proper name."

"What would I call her?" I asked
Amar thought for a few seconds, *"Enakshi is an old Sanskrit name that means the eyes of a deer."*
I thought the name was perfect as it not only defined her physically but also expressed her timid curiosity.

I felt numb as I walked over to her with my arms outstretched. She rushed towards me, threw her arms around me and cried.
"No one will ever hurt you again Enakshi." I whispered.
"Enakshi ?" she asked
"Yes…Enakshi."
She smiled at Amar as he put his hands together and nodded with approval.

As well as having a new name Ladki, now Enakshi, was about to have a new life. Amar and I agreed that we couldn't leave her there so very willingly she jumped onto the cart beside me and we set off to introduce her to her new home.

On the journey back to Amar's house I told him about my experiences in solitude. The heightened sense of memory with Charlie, the encounter with David and how I never felt alone and certainly not lonely, none of which seemed to surprise Amar. I asked him if he could explain the feeling I had when I had to cross the river to reach Enakshi. In a very matter of fact way he said, *"Don't look for an explanation just accept that you were able to do it. Enakshi isn't the only person who will call on you. There will be many as you become more aware of the help that you will be able to give."*

The rest of the twenty or so mile journey back seemed to pass quite quickly and without much conversation as I contemplated what Amar had said about my future. I wondered how I would be able to help people as he had said. How would they call me and what sort of help would I be to whoever they were? Was I to become a Spiderman or Captain America type superhero? And would I get a uniform? I smiled to myself at the ridiculous notion and noticed Enakshi smiling back. The short-lived fantasy soon dispersed into the hot Indian air as Amar's house came into view. Vimal rushed outside to greet us. He held out his hand to help Enakshi down from the cart and although she took my hand instead I could sense an instant attraction between them.

On the way into the house I could see that the old mystic and Vimal were in their usual silent conversation and I knew that Vimal was being told about Enakshi by the look of pity and concern in the young man's eyes. Although he couldn't take his eyes off Enakshi he made a point of keeping his distance. Every time she glanced back at him he slowed his pace so not to invade her space. It was like a courteous and quite humorous courtship dance.

After making sure Enakshi was settled and feeling at home I was eager to get to my room to see what the book had to tell me. Out of curiosity, when I had placed the book back after the last time I opened it I had placed part of a small spider's web across the closed pages, which would have broken had the book been opened. The web was still there so I assumed that there wasn't going to be the usual addition for me to read. I was wrong; I opened it and discovered the hand written translation next to the page of Sanskrit..

> Solitude allows the voice within you that always speaks the truth to be heard.

Like after the previous trials I wasn't expected to dive into the next one so I enjoyed being back at the house listening to the wisdom of Amar, seeing Vimal's smiling face and drawing with Enakshi. We would sit in the garden while Vimal delivered his repertoire of delicious food and fruit juices. Enakshi would sometimes help him prepare the meals and would draw little pictures, which was the way she would communicate with him. I noticed that Vimal would always stuff the drawings that Enakshi did into his tunic, never throwing any of them away. It was getting pretty obvious that they were falling in love, not just based on what I was seeing but their individual energy, that I could always sense, was uniting to form a new combined force, which was like standing in a refreshing spring rain shower every time I sensed it. Within just a couple of weeks they had invented their own sign language interspersed with Enakshi's drawings. Although it meant that I was spending less time with Enakshi it was wonderful to see how happy she was and how her relationship with Vimal was developing. Enakshi would try and encourage Vimal to draw with her but he would look at whatever she was drawing, shake his head and give her one of his very special smiles. Because of what Enakshi had experienced that day that I first found her Vimal would keep a few paces away from her as not to impose himself, which I thought was an incredibly thoughtful and respectful thing to do but one day when he took his usual step back from Enakshi she reached out, took his hand and pulled him closer. These two young people who had both suffered severe hardships throughout their lives were an inspiration to anyone who might claim physiological bad effects from experiencing hard times. They were also an inspiration to me to develop what I had gained throughout my time in India.

During the following days I would practice what I had learned in solitude and my other earlier trials. Replaying incredible vivid memories with Charlie as if I was really back with her. I could even recall memories of her as a little girl playing with her toys, not in our old house in England but I could transpose them to Amar's garden as if she was actually there beside me. I would spend hours identifying distant animals going about their lives as they exported their energy to my senses and feel the effort that a flower would make as it slowly opened to greet the morning sunlight. My heightened awareness was no longer exhausting; it refreshed, energised and fulfilled me. I was ready for my next enlightenment.

Trial 5 –Fear

"The time has come to confront your greatest anxiety."
Amar was never one to mince his words and that particular day was no exception as he expanded on his rather worrying announcement.
"When you expose yourself to your deepest fear, fear will have no power, and you will transform your fear into freedom to truly engage with your spiritual awareness."

I knew Amar wasn't referring to my slight aversion to creepy crawlies, but I hoped that he wasn't about to mention my real fear – something that had been with me since I was a little boy, the fear of being buried alive. I don't know why it scared me or where it came from but whenever I had to walk past a graveyard my pace would instinctively quicken. It wasn't a fear of death; in fact when Charlie died I felt guilty of being alive and wanted to die myself. It was the thought of confinement, darkness and suffering that freaked me out.

Amar confirmed my sneaking suspicion about him knowing my real fear.
He didn't need to mention the word burial at first as he explained, *"People are prisoners of their own fears, they are bound to them and limited by them. Your confinement will enable your spirit to break free from your isolation and only your body will remain isolated."*

Although I believed and trusted Amar, after all he hadn't been wrong up until then, this was going to be like telling someone with aquaphobia to dive off Niagara Falls or asking an arachnophobe to snog a tarantula. He then dropped the 'b' word bombshell.
"It is time to be buried now Tim."

With somewhat shaky legs I followed Amar to an area of the jungle that I had never ventured to before. In a small clearing was a freshly dug rectangular shaped hole. Amar put his hand on my shoulder and led me closer to it. Although I was, by then, pretty terrified I could feel his reassuring energy flow though my body like warm honey.

Peering down into the hole I could see a short ladder leading to an open coffin. *"Oh my God,"* I said out loud.
The lid of the coffin had a hole in it, about two centimeters in diameter and there was a hollow bamboo pole lying on the ground, which I assumed was to be my breathing mechanism.

Amar smiled and gestured for me to climb down into my worst nightmare. I didn't ask how long I was to endure this ordeal, as I didn't really want to know.

Almost immediately as I lay down the lid was closed over me and the bamboo pole appeared through the hole. As I heard the earth falling onto the top of the coffin my whole body felt wet. At first I thought that water was somehow getting in and I was about to drown until I realised panic had invaded my pores and I had become bathed in my own sweat. I had never experienced blackness like it before. My first trial of darkness when I wore the hood was never this dark. Black had just got blacker than I ever could have imagined but that extreme darkness wasn't the only new experience I was aware of. I felt there was someone with me. It wasn't at all frightening in fact it made my present, terrifying situation quite assuaging. It didn't have an energy that I could sense so it obviously wasn't Amar or David. It was just an awareness that seemed to be looking after me and since that moment that feeling has never left me. I wanted to give it a name to somehow bring it closer to me. My Hindi was getting quite fluent by now so I decided to call it Saaya, which meant shadow. The thought of a middle-aged man with an imaginary friend should be cause for concern but only the name was imaginary. I was convinced that Saaya was beside me and still is to this day. At last I had met the lifelong guide that Amar had said I would meet when I was ready.

Not feeling totally alone six feet under and in total darkness helped me to gain a degree of control of my thoughts and emotions. As I lay there I felt my breathing become normal and my muscles not so tense. Eventually I was able to think clearly and had less need for Saaya's reassuring presence. I recalled Amar's words, *"Your confinement will enable your spirit to break free from your isolation and only your body will remain isolated."*

I had nothing to loose except failure of it not

working. I knew that the out of body experiences that I had encountered before were a little scary (looking down at myself never really appealed to me) but I really wanted to free myself from my underground prison. Achieving the silence of sound and thought was pretty easy and very soon I became intoxicated with awareness. I no longer felt confined to the grave. I was traveling upwards, first through the rough earth, then the soft grass and eventually I reached the clear blue sky. I could see, hear and smell everything around me as if I was really there. I could be anywhere I wanted to be. I sat beside Enakshi as she drew a portrait of Vimal who was sitting opposite her. I knew they couldn't see me but I saw her pause for a few seconds as if she was sensing something. Was she aware of me being there? I visited Amar, who was walking back to the house; he looked up and smiled at me. Could he sense me too, or actually see me? How could this have been possible? One second I was like a bird flying above him the next I was running along the path in front of him like a dog that he was taking for a run in the jungle. Unlike recalling past memories of being with Charlie this was for real. I could be anywhere I wanted to be at the present time.

All I had to do was want to be in a certain place and I could be there. Not in an hour or even a minute but instantly. I was free and wanted to visit people that I cared about.

I first thought of Tanvi, the beautiful young woman in the burnt-out village who I had met on my journey with Bandhu. As I pictured her face I was instantly by her side. She seemed even more beautiful than when we met over a year ago. She wasn't in the village but was in a hospital wearing a white coat. She was with a group of other young people dressed the same. They were all listening to an older woman. I couldn't hear what was being said but I assumed that Tanvi had become a student doctor. I noticed that she was wearing a wedding ring. I must have concentrated on the ring as I think it caused her to touch it and smile; she seemed happy.

I next thought of the tiny temple where I first saw Ragini. Like the first time that we met she was there again arranging flowers by the ornate altar but this time it was different. Standing beside her were a young man and woman wearing wedding costumes. I knew they were Ragini's son and his bride who had lost their lives soon after they were married. I desperately tried to communicate with Ragini to tell her that she wasn't alone then I saw Ragini look confused, almost frightened but after a few seconds, without looking at the young couple, she smiled, laughed and then cried with joy. Her husband Hari then arrived with some water for the flowers. Ragini turned to him.

"They were here Hari, they were here."
"I know." Answered Hari, *"I felt them too."*
This pleased me enormously knowing that I had fulfilled my promise to Ragini and Hari to be able to sense what I could. I left them as they embraced each other.

I wanted to check on 'The Boy' but felt quite nervous about what may have become of him. Was he dealing with his terrible disfigurement, or had he again withdrawn from society and the pain that his torment had caused him in the past?

I found myself in a large tent with hundreds of people looking up at a masked trapeze artist. I knew this was 'The Boy' and although he was an amazing performer I felt saddened by him feeling the need to cover his face. I stayed with him during his incredible act and was thankful that at least he hadn't ended up in some sort of freak show, but I wanted to know where he would go after the performance. I watched the crown disperse from the tent into the night to their family homes and after a while 'The Boy' made his way to a large trailer. Inside were all the other circus people sitting down to enjoy a meal together. As 'The Boy' entered the trailer he received a loud cheer as he took off his mask and joined the party. He had found his family but what about mine?

Of course, I wanted to be with Charlie but could feel no connection or direction to take. So why was I able to see Ragini's dead son and wife and not my own child who I constantly missed and should have had a strong connection with? Where was her spirit and who or what had she become? The frustration of all this disrupted my free spirit and sent me back to my incarcerated state, six feet under. Once again all I could see was total blackness. As I lay there and thought about what I could now achieve two things sprang to mind. If I could free myself from my body due to the fear of where my body was would I be able to do it if I wasn't in a state of fear? And when my spirit was free would it be possible for me to communicate with whoever I chose to visit? There was one obvious person who I could try this on – David.

Freeing myself from my body took a little longer this time as I wasn't as scared of where I was any more but after a minute or two I felt the journey begin again – up through the dense earth and into the air above the ground. In an instant I was where my incredible journey had begun, at the bench on the southwest coast of England. It was a very dark night as I heard a familiar sound entered my senses.
"Hello Tim."
Not only could I hear him, I could see him, odd socks and all.
There was no way that I could speak but I could think the words I wanted to say. *"Hello David, can you actually hear me?"*
"Of course. As well as you can hear me."
Back in my coffin I must have been grinning like a Cheshire Cat. There I was over four thousand miles from where I actually was, having a conversation with the spirit of a dead man.

I told him how I had visited Ragini and managed to see her lost son. I asked why wasn't I able to connect with Charlie.
"She's not ready but she's listening."
"What do you mean she's not ready? Has she not been gone long enough?" I couldn't bring myself to say the word dead. *"When will I be able to see her again?"*
"You still have a long way to go on your journey and connecting with Charlie isn't your final destination."

I kind of realised what he was saying. If I could see and speak to Charlie again I would stop everything right there and then and spend the rest of my life being with her whenever I wanted to be and that obviously wasn't what the grand plan was for me.

I stayed with David until night slowly gave way to dawn's light. It was mainly a one-way conversation as I listened to David's calm and sagacious thoughts. I felt I was on more of an equal footing with him than I had been before – 'a meeting of minds' for want of a better cliché. He spoke of things so obvious that very few people even consider them.

"People believe they have their own worlds, which consists of their own lives, their own families, the job that they do and the people they call friends. Everything else is someone else's world, which means there must be millions of worlds, which everyone knows isn't true but they continue to live their lives as if it is. This is why there is pain and suffering throughout the world. The truth is, there is only one world and one family and everyone is part of it. Why does a mother have to watch her child die of starvation when another mother has food to spare? And why do two men fight each other for the love of different countries in the same world?"

David continued with a more personal example.
"A few years ago you saw a teenage girl begging in the street. Why didn't you help her?"
I answered without too much consideration.
"Because she may have just wanted money for drugs."
"But you didn't know that. She may just have been hungry. Why did you help Enakshi when she was being raped?"
"Because I knew what was happening to her."

"But why didn't you ask why the teenage girl was begging?"

I didn't need to answer the question as David answered it for me.
"Because Enakshi became part of your world and the begging girl didn't. If you had come across the girl after Charlie had become ill you would have helped her because she would have been closer to your world"

David then hit me with a metaphorical sledgehammer.
"A few weeks after you walked past the begging girl she died of hypothermia. She had left home because her stepfather was abusing her. And she had never taken drugs"
" Why did you have to tell me that?" I asked.
"Because very soon you will have one world and one family but until then you must become aware of the tiny world that you are still living in. When your trials are complete you will experience true compassion, without favouritism, for any living thing. The gift that you have will do great things once you fully accept and realise it."
"What sort of things will I do and when will this be?" I asked.

"When you stop asking questions and know the answers." He said as he left me alone in my coffin.

As I lay there I wondered what answers I would know and when and how I would know them without asking questions. Since my earliest school day memories I had been encouraged to question everything so how could it be right what David had told me? I immediately realised that I had just asked myself another question. Maybe he was right, after all since my time in India the awareness that I had gained wasn't from asking questions, it was from accepting what was happening to me, and in fact when I did question any of the teaching that Amar had made me aware of, my senses had become either disturbed, confused or temporary disconnected. Everything I had learnt was by experiencing a more intense observation of things around me and by undergoing long periods of silence and meditation and not questioning what I was discovering. Maybe the western doctrine for increasing knowledge and intellect was all wrong.

My thoughts were suddenly disturbed by a

noise on the coffin lid, which I hoped wasn't an animal trying to get in. This fear was soon put to rest when I heard Amar's voice as the lid was slowly lifted. *"Hello Tim, time to go."* At first the sudden light hurt my eyes and my legs were a little unstable.
"I think I conquered more than my fear in there," I said to Amar as we made our way back to the house.
"Being in total darkness opened my eyes to what matters outside of my small world."
Amar didn't comment, he just nodded.

As I walked back through the garden towards the house Enakshi and Vimal were sitting very close together by the rock pool. Enakshi raised her hand to wave to me then put her hand on top of Vimal's. He glanced at me looking a little guilty then smiled as I gave him a subtle nod of approval. I went straight to my room to see what the book was going to reveal, expecting the next addition to be something about conquering fear. It wasn't, instead the words echoed the thoughts of David.

*To be without favouritism
is the path to inner sense*

There were those two words again - inner sense. The two words that David had explained that I must achieve and had led me on this incredible six-year journey.

There was something different about the book this time. As I curiously turned the page I could somehow read, what had been, until that moment, a foreign language. I could now comprehend the ancient Sanskrit. It was as if someone was silently reading to me, but it was all in my own head and I could understand every word. Was this Saaya, my guardian shadow, making this possible? Or was it yet another stage of awareness that I had somehow achieved?

I spent the whole night devouring the thoughts, scriptures and poems of the profound bygone authors who had contributed to the book that was no longer a mystery to me. Ancient quotes like:

"Do your duty; learn and teach.
Speak only truth; learn and teach.
Meditate; learn and teach.
Control sense; learn and teach.
Control the mind; learn and teach.
Kindle fire: learn and teach.
Feed fire; learn and teach.
Be hospitable; learn and teach.
Be humane; learn and teach.
Serve the family; learn and teach.
Educate your children; learn and teach."

There was a poem that rang so true.

Bitter Grief
Such bitter grief as this has broken my heart,
yet it still has not burst apart.
And my body, fainting from the smart,
the senses do not depart.

Internal fires within my body blaze,
And yet I am not consumed.
Fortune has cleft me with a mortal wound,
Yet still I live out my days.

There was also a passage about reincarnation, which reminded me of my second meeting with David at the bench when he first planted the notion of the undying spirit that I was both suspicious and disbelieving of at the time. The words that filled my head this time had a greater conviction to my now more open mind. I imagined the words that I read coming from a wise old man like Amar as he spoke to a young student:

"We know that all souls reincarnate from one body into another, evolving through experience over long periods of time. Death is not fearsome. Like the caterpillar's metamorphosis into the delicate butterfly, death does not end our existence but frees us to pursue an even greater existence. The soul never dies. It is immortal. Physical death is a most natural transition for the soul, which survives and guided by karma, continues its long pilgrimage. Reincarnation is the natural cycle of birth, death & rebirth. When we die, the soul leaves the first world physical body, it lives for a while in the Devaloka, the Second World, before returning again to earth in the Bhuloka or first world.

In the Devaloka the mind, emotions and associations continue. There is no escape from life's experiences. We must re-experience the karma that we have created, be it joyous, painful or mixed. Thus turns the slow wheel of samsara.

We know that because of the law of karma we will have to be born again and again to reap the fruits of all actions, good, bad and mixed. How then do we stop the process? Understanding the way karma is, we naturally seek to live a good and virtuous life through right speech and right action. When one thinks, speaks and acts correctly, one feels good about oneself, for we are then living in harmony with the whole of creation, expressing the higher qualities of our own divine soul. We perform an action without expecting or wanting anything in return. When all actions are mentally surrendered we attain purity of heart and mind.

In this way actions and their reactions good, bad or mixed dissolve and mental freedom and inner peace is maintained. Thus, one of the goals of life is experienced and painful karmas are not created to be re-experienced at a later time.

We believe that we are not our physical body

but live within it as a divine and perfect immortal soul. We believe that the end of birth does not begin and end in a single life but that this process is continuous, reaching beyond the limits that one life may impose. The law of karma assures one of a better birth if life has been lived virtuously. We also know that if one does not live an ethical life, suffering will come in a future life.

The belief in karma and reincarnation brings to each of us inner peace and self-assurance. We know that the maturing of the soul takes many lives and that if the soul is immature in the present birth then there is hope, for there will be many opportunities for learning and growing in future lives. These beliefs and attitudes produce eliminate anxiety, giving the serene perception that everything is all right as it is. There is no sense of a time limit, of impending judgment of actions and attitudes in our mind. And there is also a remarkable insight into the human condition and appreciation for all men in all stages of spiritual unfoldment."

Shortly after I put the book down I must have dozed off as a loud clap of thunder, which seemed to shake the whole building, suddenly woke me up. Lightning lit the room brighter than daylight followed by another loud bang less than a second after. The storm was obviously directly overhead.

I made my way to the garden, to get a better look and had to cover my ears to soften the sound of the rain, like a million machine guns hitting the wooden roof. As I approached the kitchen door leading to the garden I could just make out, through the blur of the torrential downpour, a figure outside. When I got to the open doorway I could see it was Amar standing with his arms outstretched. Each bolt of lightning gave him a ghostly appearance. I called out to him. *"Amar be careful, it's dangerous."*
Still with arms wide he turned to me.
"Join me Tim. Feel the energy."

Without hesitation I walked out into the raging storm. Amar took my hand and held our joined hands above our heads. I raised my other hand to mirror his posture as we both stood motionless. The rain, lightning and thunder massaged all my senses and I felt like I needed to shout loud. My Hindi was by now fluent and the word that came into my head was *"adhik, adhik'* (more, more) Amar joined in with his own chant. *"Dhanyavaad, dhanyavaad"* (thank you, thank you).

I glanced back at the house and as another flash of lightning lit up the garden I saw something that made me feel very happy, the naked silhouettes of Vimal and Enakshi though Vimal's bedroom window. I changed my chant to Amar's *"dhanyavaad."* Was I thanking the storm for allowing me to see their happiness or expressing my gratitude to whatever one of their Gods had brought them together? Whichever it was I will never forget that moment.

The storm left as dawn arrived leaving everything refreshed, including me. Still standing in the garden with Amar he said quietly, *"you're ready for your final trial."*

Trial 6 –Death

Amar led me to a room in the house that I had never been in before. I had sometimes wondered what was behind the door but it always seemed locked even though there was no keyhole. I just took it for granted that it was an unused room and time had made the door stick. Effortlessly Amar gently pushed the door open to reveal a dark interior with no windows and a high vaulted ceiling. There was a smell of old wood, not unpleasant but very descriptive of the age of the room. Every inch of the walls were carved with elaborate figures and symbols. Various columns, also with complex carvings, reached high into the vaulted ceiling and disappeared into the darkness. The place resembled a temple or crypt. There was no furniture except for a small table on tall stilt-like legs in the middle of the room, lit only by the open door. On the table was a small brass cup. Amar took the cup and gave it to me. Inside was a tiny amount of bright purple liquid.

"Drink this Tim and your journey will be complete. All that you have learnt and discovered will join together to give you the inner sense."

A rush of excitement filled my head. This is it, I thought. Everything that had been promised was now going to happen. Having complete

faith in Amar, as usual, I drank the liquid that tasted sweeter than anything that I had ever tasted before.
I waited for an instant enlightenment, but nothing happened.

"What happens now?' I asked.
"You will die," answered Amar calmly.
"You mean that was poison?"
As I said poison I could feel my world spinning out of control. Amar became a blur as my breathing became shallow. I felt my heart stop in my chest. The last thought in my head was…why?

This was instantly replaced by an incredible sensation. I had heard about people having near death experiences, describing traveling along bright tunnels or being engulfed in light and feeling very happy but this was nothing like that. I was in a totally different world, way beyond description to the human perception. It wasn't a bright, warm place or a black hole. It was a non-dimensional limbo. I could feel neither warmth nor cold. The most overwhelming feeling was being stripped naked of any kind of discrimination or opinion. I was incapable of being what I thought was me. It was a feeling of complete tolerance. Everything that I had learnt over the last six years joined together in a sudden rush of intensity. I was a butterfly breaking out of a chrysalis, a bud bursting into a flower, a baby taking its first gulp of air, yet although I was experiencing the feeling of being born, I had an intense awareness of history. Not just my own bygone years but also those of every spirit that had occupied a living form.

I was free from confusion, guilt, doubt, judgment and the most liberating thing of all - time. I wasn't governed by it and had no desire or concern about returning to the life I once had. I knew I was on a journey and to define the feeling as euphoric was an inadequate description. I had no questions to ask as Saaya, who was guiding me, was answering everything for me. Not in a Charles Dickens 'ghost of Christmas past' way. Saaya wasn't leading me by the hand through my murky past. What I was discovering was the truth, without insularity, about the world I once lived in. I could see why certain human beings had made the decisions that had led to intolerance and suffering.

I entered the minds of past perpetrators of war, famine, genocide and torture and discovered a common belief in the minds of these agents of evil that none considered themselves guilty or repentant of any crime. They were all convinced that what they had done would result in a better outcome for themselves and for the countries they honoured. Some even felt closer to their god because of their actions. They believed it was justified to destroy lives to preserve others similar to their own. My spirit was free to connect with a young man in Germany - a talented artist and part of a Bohemian community. I stayed with him and observed his growing obsession for power, which enabled the destruction of over fifty million human beings due to his personal paranoia of a race of people that became an epidemic of fear throughout his country. His own people called him my leader - in their language Mein Führer. I perceived his spirit leave his body some years later and become trapped in the complexities of Karma where it still remains, unable to enter another life form.

As well as entering the minds of the executors of suffering I also became the victims. My first experience was to feel bodies pressed close to mine. It was incredibly hot and there was a strong smell of sweat and blood. I felt a tight pain around my wrist and as I looked down I saw that my skin was black and a steel shackle joined me to the wrist of another man. I was an African, stolen from my home and on board a ship to be sold as a slave. The sound that emanated through the dim light was a mixture of moans, crying and defiant singing. This was suddenly interrupted by a shout in Portuguese from a crewmember. He said there was a storm coming and the ship had to lose some ballast. Me and fifty other African men and women were to become that ballast. I felt a tug on my chains as I was pulled from below deck and led outside. Weights were attached to our legs and we were thrown overboard. I hit the water and felt a huge sense of freedom as I took a gulp of seawater into my lungs – everything then went into total darkness.

I was then a young boy of the Lakota Sioux tribe. It was December 29 1890 in South Dakota. I was playing with friends on our reservation. I heard gunshots and ran back to the village. Soldiers were killing everyone - old people, women and children; I felt a burning pain in my side followed by another in my chest and saw my own blood cover my body before I fell to the ground. I heard my mother call my name: "White Eagle, White Eagle." She fell beside me as a bullet went through her head. The pain disappeared as my spirit left my body. I could see the bodies of over two hundred and fifty of my tribe, mostly women and children, lying next to my own human form. I felt no anger even though a few weeks later I saw twenty of the soldiers being awarded their county's Medal of Honour for their "bravery."

Saaya brought me forward seventy-eight years later to a village called My Lai in Vietnam. It was early one morning and I was an old woman feeding some pigs in a small enclosure next to my bamboo thatched house that I shared with my family of two daughters, their husbands and four children. Soldiers appeared from everywhere. Although they were wearing different uniforms to the ones in Dakota back in 1890 their faces looked the same. Contorted with rage and hatred they started firing bullets into everyone. Some people pleaded with them only to end up getting shot at close range. Young women were dragged from their houses and raped as other soldiers watched and waited for their turn.

When the women could take no more, they were shot. I was told to stand in a ditch with about thirty other women and children. An officer called to a young soldier, *"gun them down,"* but the soldier threw his weapon on the ground and cried. The officer picked up the machine gun and started firing into us shouting, *"filthy Cong,"* and *"VC scrum."* As bullets ripped into me I watched our village being burnt to the ground and, like us, our animals mercilessly slaughtered.

During the same year and less than a month later I was sitting, next to a radio, in a small room in Alabama late in the evening. I was an eighty-year-old black man. One by one members of my family joined me next to the radio as we listened to a gospel choir singing:

"Hold on
Just a little while longer
Hold on
Just a little while longer
Hold on
Just a little while longer

Everything will be alright

Fight on
just a little while longer
Fight on
just a little while longer
Pray on
just a little while longer

Everything will be alright

Sing on
Just a little while longer
Sing on
Just a little while longer
Sing on
Just a little while longer

Everything will be alright
Everything will be alright."

There was a short pause after the song finished then a solemn sounding DJ said, *"a fitting tribute to Martin Luther King Junior who was assassinated earlier this evening."*

Unlike my time buried alive in the coffin I was unable to choose where I wanted to go. I was just taken - to experience every kind of human suffering that was dealt out by other human beings. I endured the most horrendous afflictions throughout history but I felt no anger, just extreme sadness. I had perished in death camps, died from starvation in China in 1959. I had felt the terror of certain annihilation and shared injustice. The way, so called, intelligent man treats his fellow man is more savage than anything in the animal world. Years before I remember watching a TV programme about blues music in Louisiana. An old singer called Lazy Lester said, *"the Devil got the blame for a lot of stuff he had nothing to do with."*

I tasted a bitter sensation on my lips followed by a sudden pain in my chest as my heart restarted and I knew I was coming back. Enakshi was standing over me holding a small cup containing what was left of the liquid I had just swallowed – the antidote to what had poisoned me and had led to my death. Although I had experienced hundreds of years of history nothing had changed, and I knew that I had only been dead for a few seconds. I didn't need to know how this was possible as I already knew the answer - spiritual experience isn't restricted to time as we know it.

I somehow knew that it was essential to have suffered the amount of pain that I had if I was to gain the inner sight and although my mind was swimming in a state of semi consciousness, I felt a huge sense of empowerment. I had no idea how this would manifest itself but from that moment I was convinced that a different and better world was possible.

Although my head became clear my legs were slow to accept that I wasn't dead any longer, so Enakshi led me back to my room where I slept for almost twenty-four hours. When I woke the first thing that hit me was a sort of emptiness. The powerful energy that always dominated the house had gone. The second thing I became aware of was the sound of crying. I went outside to the garden to see Vimal being comforted by Enakshi. It was ironic to hear the only voice that ever came from Vimal's mouth was the sound that accompanied his tears. Although I already knew the answer to the question I was about to ask, I asked it any way.
"What's wrong, what's happened," I

whispered to Enakshi.
"Amar has died," she said.

Chapter 3

Amar had been laid out on his bed. The subtle smile that he always displayed was still there. I so wanted to connect with him but I knew his spirit was far from my reach. From that moment I believed that he had achieved Moksha – The Hindu belief of freedom from Samsara, the cycle of death and rebirth. Amar had gained perfect peace beyond any human understanding. I returned to my room and opened the last page of the book. The final entry was from the amazing man himself.

I have fulfilled my quest and you now have the gift of inner sight to accomplish great acts of compassion that will contribute to a better world.
You have a great responsibility to pursue peace and harmony wherever your guide takes you.
It is limitless in what you can achieve.

In true Hindu tradition we lit a candle and placed it by Amar's head. When the candle had burnt out Vimal shaved Amar's body, anointed it in sandalwood oil and he and Enakshi wrapped the body in linen. We placed Amar in the entrance to the house with his head facing south. At dusk Vimal and I carried his body to a clearing in the jungle and placed it on a funeral pyre. Enakshi said a prayer to Yama, the god of death. Before Vimal lit the fire he removed the ruby ring on Amar's finger and placed it on mine, which, I felt was a great honour. We stayed there all night in complete silence and meditation.

The next ceremony, a few months later, wasn't as solemn. I gave Enakshi away to be Vimal's wife. It was a great pleasure, second only to watching Charlie being born. Before that day I was experiencing some very deep feelings of concern for what was happening in the world outside of that idyllic place that I called home. It was as though I was being called away by a force almost as strong as when I first rescued Enakshi. I resisted what I knew I would have to succumb to until after the wedding.

On the morning of the wedding I knew Vimal was worried about marrying Enakshi. I went deeper into his concerns and sensed that he was having second thoughts – not about his love for his future bride but whether he was worthy of her. Would he be able to be the husband that she deserved because of his inability to hear or speak? That was when I discovered the gift that I now had. I spoke to Vimal, not through telepathy but through his own thoughts. I was able to allow him to reassess his own concerns and make him realise that marrying the woman he loved would be the right decision. I saw the look on his face change to a confident smile and it was at that point that I knew what I was capable of and that I had to leave soon after the wedding to put my gift to good use.

A little later a priest arrived from the nearest

village to perform the ceremony, which lasted all day – short by Hindu standards as they usually go on for at least three days with numerous guests but as I was the only person, other than the bride and groom, it would have been difficult to string it out for that long. Enakshi looked beautiful in her traditional red wedding dress that she had made herself and Vimal stood so upright and proud throughout the whole ceremony I thought his back was going to seize up.

I wanted to experience their feeling for each other for just a few seconds so I trespassed into their thoughts and felt a love so strong it made me, uncontrollably, burst out laughing. Enakshi and Vimal turned towards me and started laughing too as did the priest who clapped his hands with joy. I couldn't have wished for a better going away present.

The next morning the three of us had breakfast together.
"What are you going to be doing with your lives?" I asked Enakshi.
"We will look for work in Varanasi to earn enough money to open an art school somewhere. I will teach and Vimal will

prepare the food, which we will grow ourselves so the fees we will charge can be very low. I will only need enough money for materials. It will be for students who can't afford the fees at expensive art colleges."

"Fantastic idea," I said, *"but why don't you do it here?"*
"What about you?" said Enakshi.
"I will be leaving today; I have some work to do and anyway the house is yours now."
"Really?" shrieked Enakshi as she jumped to her feet, causing Vimal to look somewhat startled. She told Vimal, through their unique sign language, what I had just said and they both hugged each other as they jumped up and down. She then looked sad when the thought of me leaving her finally sank in.

To avoid an emotional goodbye I left that afternoon while Enakshi and Vimal were walking in the jungle. I set off along the narrow dusty road and it wasn't long before I was able to hitch a ride with one of the locals on his ox cart. He was going to Narad Ghat, which was fine with me, as I didn't have a clue where I wanted to go. I didn't need to spend any money on food as I soon discovered that

something amazing was about to happen. It started when I arrived in Narad Ghat. An old woman greeted me with a namaste and beckoned me to follow her to a small house on the steps facing the Ganges. She went into the house and reappeared with a basket of food, which she gave me, then put her hands together and bowed her head again before going back into her house. As I sat by the river to enjoy my free meal, a little confused about what had just happened, I heard David's voice. I looked around but couldn't see him.
"People will find you and help you to go where your guide takes you. Don't question them, just thank them for their kindness and understanding with these words." I listened carefully as the words *"aap duniya ko dete hain"* filled my head. I knew that it meant *"you give to the world"* but I didn't know exactly how they were giving to the world or what in the world it would be.

It started with a journey to Paradip, a port on the east coast of India. I was to board a cargo ship to Shanghai. I didn't know why I knew that's where I was going or what I was going for, I just knew. I decided to set off early the next day after sleeping in a disused shack by the river. The journey was over five hundred miles and took the whole of the following day and some of the evening. Various modes of transport took me there ranging from local buses to tuk-tuks. I never had to pay a single rupee for the whole of the journey - the last stage of which was by taxi that I didn't have to hail. The driver just stopped and offered a free ride. He didn't say a word all of the way, but he smiled as I put my hands together and said, *"aap duniya ko dete hain,"* when I got out at Paradip. I was never short of food either. People just appeared and gave it to me, which was kind of strange at first but the more it happened the more I just accepted it as if it was now the normal thing to happen. And each time there was an act of kindness I acknowledged it with *"aap duniya ko dete hain"* and a smiling namaste was received in return.

When I got to the port I was welcomed by a very different smell of India. The familiar fragrance of spices and garbage was blended with heavy fuel oil and rotting marine life, which was amplified to maximum effect by the intense heat. The ship that I was to travel to Shanghai on was already being loaded with its cargo of brass vases in all shapes and sizes, badly carved figures, dried herbs and brightly patterned rugs to name just a few of anything that the Chinese might be interested in buying.

I approached a young man who was supervising the loading and asked him if I could work my passage to Shanghai. I didn't want to own up to having any money. Appearing to be penniless was safer in this part of the country. Without eye contact or any hint of an expression he asked me if I had any experience on cargo ships.

I now had two options: do I claim to have sailed the seven seas for thirty plus years, fighting off pirates and discovering uncharted islands or do I own up to be a complete land lubber not knowing my port from my starboard or if I had to splice the main brace I had no idea where to find it or how to spice it if it was pointed out to me? I decided that honesty was the best policy but said that I was prepared to do whatever nautical skivvying was below the skills of the other experienced salty sea dogs. The young man just shook his head and turned away.

I then sensed a strong, positive energy coming from the ship and as I looked up I saw that an older man was looking down at me.

"Namaste," he said as he made his way down the rickety old gangplank.

"I am the captain. The journey will take almost three weeks - we sail in two hours and there is no need for you to work. You are welcome."

The young man shrugged his shoulders in disbelief and stepped aside to allow me to board. *"Aap duniya ko dete hain"* I said to the captain as I passed him. He smiled with a slight bow of his head.

"Please have dinner with me after we sail."

I gratefully accepted mainly because I wanted to know why he was being so accommodating and how he seemed to know who I was.

That evening I dined on Fish Aksal at the captain's table, which wasn't exactly a table but actually a sheet of ply board on top of an old packing crate and two rusty metal fold-down chairs facing each other. The meal wasn't great, especially compared with the food that Vimal had prepared for me during my time at Amar's house. The cabin was small to say the least with a single mattress on the floor and a corner desk with a few navigational instruments on it. It was luxurious in comparison to my cabin though– the size of a broom cupboard with a hammock slung across the full length of the room with a porthole about the size of a cricket ball. The captain's English was very good as he told his interesting story. His father was an Indian diplomat who had married a Japanese opera singer hence his striking mixed Asian looks. When he was a young man he had rebelled against his father's wishes to join the diplomatic corps and joined the merchant navy to see the world on his own terms. He said he always had the ability to feel people's energy, which was why he was able to sense mine. *"You have a powerful presence,"* he said. *"That is why I wanted to know more about you."*

I thought it was beyond coincidence that he had the ability to sense what I could, but I had no reason to be suspicious, as no one had told me to travel on his ship, I just knew I had to.

At first, I was cautious to reveal my adventures and the enlightenment I had gained over the past six years but after a few more meals together during my twenty days at sea I could see that he was genuinely interested in what I had to tell and I was keen to tell it to someone who was believing every word. He didn't seem to doubt even the most bizarre parts of my story, which cemented our friendship even more. Before every meal the captain would select an old seventy-eight rpm record from a wooden trunk and place it on a 1950's Dansette Major record player. His choice was always sitar music by Ustad Vilayat Khan, the greatest musician ever, as I was told. We would both speak very quietly as if to respect the tranquility of the music. Our voices became like an accompaniment and we would find ourselves talking in a spontaneous rhythm to the sitar.

I believe we all have our own personal audio library full of different sounds that we can call upon and listen to whenever a certain memory provokes it. The sound of a loved ones voice, a pleasant bird song in a favourite place or a child's laughter. The sitar music went into my library and from that time on I became a regular borrower.

During the last night of the journey and yet another average fish dinner the captain said: *"Would you allow me to tell your story? I'm a very keen writer."*

"My story doesn't have an ending yet." I said, *"And in any case I'm not sure that anyone would believe it so if you were to write it you had better do it as fiction."* He laughed and said, *"Will you come back to tell me how your story ends, if indeed it ever does?"*

"I will, even if it doesn't have an ending I'll come back. I promise."

"Thank you – and I hope that you find Charlie. I think you will."

The next day we arrived at the port of Shanghai where the captain and I parted company. Up until then we hadn't had any physical contact but as I went to shake his hand I felt an incredible sense of truth, trust and awareness. It also filled me with hope and encouragement just when I needed it, as I wasn't sure what lay ahead on the next part of my journey or why I was about to embark on it anyway.

When I reached the stern looking border control officer I just looked at him. I didn't know why I did it, I just did. I stared into his eyes until he looked confused. His eyes half glazed over before taking a step back and letting me through without asking for any documentation. Did I somehow hypnotise him? I don't know, as I had never done anything like that before, but it continued to work on all of my future travels. Like people giving me free food, that kind of thing just happened.

After clearing customs I had no hesitation in terms of the direction I needed to take. Saaya guided me to the centre of the city to The People's Square. There was a large gathering of students there, facing about fifty armed soldiers. I could sense a multitude of emotions: anger, frustration, pride and the most powerful of all - fear.

Up until that moment I could sense any living body's energy but that was all. I was able to feel what they were feeling. I could even switch my awareness to each individual person if I chose to but what good would that do? They would still be out to harm or even kill each other. This time I needed to, somehow, control their energy and influence the outcome of a situation that was destined for disaster.

I soon became focused on the young officer in command who was obsessed with a sense of duty and responsibility that was facing him. His thoughts were full of nothing else but the job he was there to do -an admirable state of mind for a soldier but potentially catastrophic for the young students that were advancing on his men, armed only with placards, baseball bats and a few firecrackers. The officer's determined energy became stronger as both groups of young people approached each other. I called on everything that Amar had taught me. I had to have faith in my ability to change things. I let go of my own senses and entered the officer's emotions. I could feel his tenacity and the grip on his pistol as he marched forward. He raised his gun and pointed it at the student leader's head but then his grip loosened as he began to stop reacting and began to feel compassion. I was communicating with him - forcing him, at first, to see an alternative and after a few seconds I didn't need to force him anymore. He knew what was about to happen was wrong. His view of the opposition changed. He could now only see and feel innocent human beings, the same age as himself. He holstered his gun and knelt to the ground with his head bowed ready to take a blow from the student leaders baseball bat.

I now had to control the student leader's energy, which was much more difficult as he was driven by passion not duty. He was there to lay his life on the line for a belief, not an obligation enforced by swearing an oath. His was a far stronger energy to influence. As he raised his bat above the officer's head in preparation to strike I could feel his eyes bulge in his head as he summoned up hate and anger. But he stopped. He looked back at his friends and he shook his head. He put the bat down and held out his hands to help the officer to his feet. All of the soldiers and the students lowered their heads in thought before laying their weapons on the ground. They stood in silence together for a full two minutes before dispersing in various directions.

I sat on the cobbled ground of the square exhausted, relieved and fulfilled. I remembered what David had said to me during our second meeting. *"You have to let go Tim."* And that's exactly what I had done. I had let go of myself to be able to become someone else, and the wonderful thing was neither the officer nor the student knew it was me. They believed it was themselves who had realised there was a much better option than violence, and they were right to believe it was themselves because it was true. Years before that day I had listened to an interview on the radio with a Reiki master about the ancient art of hands-on healing. She said a Reiki healer doesn't heal people, they just open the necessary channels for them to heal themselves and that was what I had done, enabled those young people to change their own minds. Things were about to become incredibly rewarding for me at last.

I wanted to leave Shanghai as soon as possible. After living in the Indian countryside for so long, city life wasn't agreeing with me.

The vacant look on the faces of people going about their stressed and structured lives reminded me too much of my own past, squashed into London tube trains thinking only of how to keep my job, protect myself from the guy trying to steal it from me and earn more money to put into a pension fund that was never going to reward me with the lifestyle that I thought I longed for.

I'd heard of a place about five hours drive away from Shanghai called Gongyu, known as the land of the inner peace. That's the place for me I thought – somewhere to meditate, reflect and try and make sense of what I was experiencing. I had no problem hitching a ride to the nearest road to the village, which from there was only accessible on foot, so I set off eagerly to discover my inner peace but unfortunately that was also the plan of herds of loud, gap-year hikers.

It was indeed a beautiful place. The morning mist was slipping off the sculptural steep rocks as I arrived at an area called the White Holy Dragon Waterfall. If it hadn't been for a fashionista's dream collection of designer labels displayed on the western invaders T-shirts and backpacks I may have stayed for some time but I left after a couple of hours and headed north following the East China Sea coast road. Again, somehow, I knew where I was supposed to go. My spiritual satnav, Saaya, was guiding me to my next venture into unfamiliar territories.

After almost a whole day of walking, accepting rides from complete strangers and even a sampan ferry crossing I arrived at Tiantai Mountain.

I didn't know why I was there, neither did I care because it was the most beautiful area that I had ever seen and I was quite happy to be part of it. Covering an area of about 72 square miles, it was a paradise of wild plants that have survived there for centuries. Palm blossoms from the time of the Sui Dynasty back in the 580's, camphor trees that had been around since the Tang Dynasty, used for treating everything from toothache to eczema, old rhododendron trees displaying their spring flowers that coated the mountain like a pink mist and an abundance of herbs.

There were also wild animals that I had never seen before and didn't even know existed. Civets that looked like foxes designed by a committee, serows that resembled a cross between a goat and an antelope and the most beautiful of all, clouded leopards, the smallest of the big cats with distinctive cloud-like patterned coats. Not much is known about them, as they are elusive and very rarely seen but I saw one of those magnificent creatures. It appeared out of the dense undergrowth into a small clearing where I had stopped for a rest. It was about the size of a North American puma and a hundred times more beautiful. I later learnt that it must have been a male as it was about 100 centimetres tall. I saw him a second or two before he saw me. When he did see me, he stood and stared as if allowing me to witness his rare appearance. He slowly turned full circle displaying his unique markings and then raised his head before standing motionless, making me feel humbled like a peasant in the presence of royalty. After a few more seconds he walked unafraid through the clearing and disappeared into the forest. From that day to this if ever I start to get above myself, thinking I'm important, I think about that privileged experience of seeing him and my own importance pales in comparison.

Saaya guided me to the Guoqing Temple, the most stunning architectural complex that I have ever visited, which is reputed to be a significant area of Chinese and Japanese Buddhism. There was an instant feeling of calm about the place, enhanced by the smell of incense burnt in large stone cauldrons inside pagodas and the gentle sound of chants that continued throughout the day and night, emanating from the various six hundred rooms. I was greeted by a young monk who showed me to my room. By now I didn't question how he knew I was arriving, I just accepted it. This was where I was to recharge my batteries, be at peace with the world and experience a feeling of complete calm, purity, awareness and honesty for the next six weeks before I was urged to travel yet again.

Most mornings I would wake around six o'clock and spend the rest of the day in meditation or exploring the many surprising finds to discover around the temple but on this particular morning I woke at four a.m. knowing I was going on another journey. I was torn between leaving and the temptation of staying in that peaceful, perfect heaven but I knew I had to go. As I left the main entrance a small group of monks were waiting for me. They each put their hands together raised them to their foreheads and said in unison, *"Sukhi Hotu"* meaning, may you be happy and well always. I couldn't have been happier where I already was but I knew I didn't have a choice. As I crossed the small stone bridge leaving

Guoqing Temple behind me I heard the distant roar of my leopard as if calling goodbye.

I still had plenty of money, thanks to Dad's inheritance, and after six more days of travel on various modes of transport I was in New York City sitting in a subway train carriage going from 57th Street Manhattan to Brownsville Brooklyn without a clue as to why.

Sitting a few seats away from me was a middle-aged woman flicking through a magazine that she wasn't really looking at and certainly wasn't reading. I could sense an extreme sadness in her eyes that I wanted to know more about. After a few more minutes of observation and hesitation I entered her thoughts. What I discovered was heartbreaking.

She was back in the past playing with a young boy of about ten years old in Central Park. I could see that everything wasn't quite normal because the boy was playing like a three-year-old and getting some strange and unsympathetic looks from a few passers by. Mum didn't care at all as they were both having great fun together. After a while they sat down on the grass. The boy waited eagerly, clapping his hands, as his mum took two bagels from a bag. She handed one to the boy and occasionally cleaned his mouth with a tissue as he enjoyed his lunch. They were both walking towards a school bus stop. There were a few other kids waiting for the bus and the boy called out to them, *"hi"* the other kids ignored the boy and turned away. The woman kissed the boy on the cheek as the bus arrived. She helped him onto the bus, waited for the door to close then walked away and started to cry. Her next memory was Coney Island. They were riding a roller coaster with their arms raised above their heads and laughing. As I looked across at the woman on the subway train there was a slight hint of a smile, which almost instantly returned to utter sadness. I feared the worse that the boy was no longer alive. I wasn't wrong.

I continued to invade her thoughts and next saw her and the boy, who was now a young man in his late teenage or early twenties, in their small apartment. She was putting a bagel, a couple of cookies and a drink into his lunch box. The young man took the box, kissed the woman and set off wearing workman's overalls.

And then she recalled her most powerful memory of all, that was easy for me to sense as she played back the past word for word.

She answered the door to a male and female police officers.
"Mrs Ellis?"
"Yes."
"May we come in?"
"Yes, it's not Eddy is it?"
"I'm afraid so."
"Is he ok?"
"Best that you sit down Ma'am."
"Is he hurt...has someone hurt him?"
"What's your first name Mrs Ellis?
"Shelly."
"Shelly...I'm sorry but your son has been killed."
"No, no, not my Eddy – why?"
"He was doing his job, cleaning up the park when he saw a gang beating up a kid. Eyewitnesses said the gang were trying to get the kid to do a drug run but the kid refused and said he was going to call a cop, so they started beating him. Eddy ran over to try and stop

them and got knifed. He was a hero ma'am...a hero."

I looked across at her still staring at the magazine. How could I stop something that had already happened? I so wanted to comfort her in some way but I knew it would freak her out if I leant across and told her what I knew, so I tried to communicate the way that I did with Vimal before he married Enakshi – through thought. I concentrated on silently speaking to her.

"Hello Shelly, this is someone on the train who knows about your love for your boy Eddy and what you're going through after losing him."

She looked around, confused but obviously keen to hear more.
I knew it was working so I continued.
"The truth is he isn't lost; his spirit is very much alive."
She looked around trying to figure out where the voice in her head was coming from. Her eyes widened as she continued to listen.

I told her about Karma and explained that if someone had led a good life and had created good Karma they will be rewarded in the next life and their spirit will go on to do great things. I spoke about how Eddy had never done anything to hurt anyone throughout his life and had only done good things despite his disability and how his spirit is pure and good.

She stopped looking around and sat back and smiled, then mouthed the words, *"thank you"* as a tear ran down her cheek. My own eyes started to well up, so I moved further down the carriage as not to be found out.

I thought that particular journey had served its purpose but I soon realised that it hadn't as I was still compelled to continue on to Brownsville, which I was soon to discover was one of the roughest areas of New York. If the thought of that wasn't bad enough my destination was to be the shittiest, most dangerous neighbourhood in that area of Brooklyn. I left the train at Rockaway Avenue station. Anyone in their right mind would have got back on the train and breathed a sigh of relief but this was where I was supposed to go.

I thought my inner guide was taking the piss when I was led to a bar called Toni's, the roughest looking place I had ever seen and that was just the outside. It was about as inviting as a rabid Rottweiler. Inside was worse than I had anticipated. What I immediately sensed wasn't good. Aggression, hate and corruption all rolled into one powerful force of energy that was coming from the back of the dimly lit room. Four guys sitting round a table, each one of them capable of scaring the shit out of any person that was stupid enough to walk into their territory, and I was that person. Was this to be my greatest challenge or my last one I thought? At first, I didn't even know why I was there but after just a few seconds it all fell into place as I kept hearing the voice of Shelly Ellis in my head. These were the guys who had killed her boy Eddy.

One of them spoke. *"Who the fuck is this piece a shit?"*
It was more or less the welcome I was expecting.
"You a cop?"
"No I'm not."
"Oh don't the piece a shit talk nice?"
So, what now I thought? Do I claim to be a James Cagney type gangster and persuade them that there is a better life than crime? Or

do I do a Steven Seagal and beat the crap out of all of them. Neither of those options were feasible so I just said, *"I've come to talk to you about Eddy."*
"Who the fuck is Eddy?" said another one of them.
"The guy you killed in Fort Greene Park."
"You talking about the retard that didn't know how to mind his own fucking business when we had some shit goin' down?"
*"No I'm talking about a youn*g man who never did anything wrong in his *life and you murdered him."*

The first guy stood up and said, *"And what the fuck are you going to do about it asswipe?"*
"I'm going to let you feel the way his mother feels."

What I was doing was completely spontaneous. If I had thought about it, I would have been convinced that it wouldn't work and I would have been shot, stabbed or both. I knew I was able to share Shelly's grief and feel what she was feeling so why not try and pass it on to the people who had killed her boy?

I just stood and looked at them. These weren't like the soldiers or the students in Shanghai motivated by duty and belief. They were driven by instinct, cold and compassionless that was in them from birth and had developed into a survival of the strongest and most ruthless. This was going to be like trying to knock down a wall with a feather. I replayed Shelly's memories in my own thoughts and focussed on her love and her loss. The pain was as unbearable as it gets; so much so that it combined with my own memories of losing Charlie. It was the second most difficult thing I had done in my life trying to deal with someone else's grief when you're still trying to deal with your own. The first most difficult thing I had ever endured was carrying my own daughter's coffin. I started to tremble; the feeling was so strong I thought I might pass out. I looked into the eyes of each of the gang members and started to transmit the pain. Nothing happened instantly but slowly they started to change their expression.

"What the fuck is goin' on?" said one of them.
"Shit man, what's happenin' here?" said another.
"You feelin' it?" asked the first guy.

"Yeah man I'm feeling it. What the fuck is it?"
"This fuckin' hurts man."
The first guy looked at me. All of his aggression had been replaced with confusion.
"Are you doin' this man?"
"Yes," I replied.
"How come? You some kind of fuckin' hypnotist or something?"
"No I'm just passing on the pain that you caused to a mum who has lost everything that she lived for."
He took a step back and said, *"How can you do that?"*
"It's a long story."
"Is it possible for someone to hurt that much?" he asked.
"Oh yes - and more."
"Shit…and we caused that hurt?"
"Yes you did."
"So what's your beef man? You tellin' us to stop the way we make a livin' by dealin' the dust?"
"No… I'm not telling you what to do; I'm just letting you feel what you've caused. What you do about it is down to you."
"So if we let you walk out of here where you gonnna' go?
"I don't know – wherever I need to go."

"To the cops?"
"No."
"Then you can go…but before you do, how do we get to know more about what you know?"
"Well, you can start by not killing people."

And with that I left; me with my life and them questioning their future, which was all I could have done.

From there I made my way to the Mahayana Buddhist Temple on Canal Street at the foot of the Manhattan Bridge. Although it was a world away from the beautiful surroundings of the Guoqing Temple on Tiantai mountain in China it was still a welcome sanctuary from mad Manhattan.

I was only planning to stay the night but like the previous seven years of my life, that hadn't quite gone according to plan, I stayed for the next two years. This was because I kept finding people who needed help, or they kept finding me.

It started the morning after I arrived, just when I was about to leave. I had no compulsion to go anywhere in particular. Saaya must have gone into sleep mode, so I thought I would try and make my way back to England to try and start some sort of new life, although I really wanted to return to India. As I left through the temple door I felt an energy that seemed to be stopping me from going. I turned to look who or what it was but there was no one there. I stood and tried to try and understand what the magnetic-like force was. The energy was getting stronger and felt very inviting.

I heard a woman's voice. *"Can I talk to you?"* Out of the shadow of the doorway stepped a young woman. She was wearing saffron and burgundy coloured robes and her head was shaved. She looked to be in her late thirties and was incredibly beautiful.
"Yes of course." I said.
"I saw you arrive yesterday and I had an instant feeling of trust in you – something that is very rare," she said. *"And a moment ago you couldn't see me but you knew I was here. How did you know that? My name is Kamiko."*
"Hi, I'm Tim. Do you want the short or the long answer?"
"I would love to hear the long one?"

She sat down on a nearby bench and I sat down beside her. I smiled and said: *"The last time I sat on an old bench with someone I didn't know, it changed my life."*
"How was that?" she asked.
"His name was David and he wasn't really there at all."
"Really? Tell me more."
"Before I do I want to know about you and what you know about me."
"All I know is what I feel," she said. *"I have only felt such a presence from my old teacher in Japan."*

We spoke for about two hours. She was born in a small village near Yokohama and had lived there until she was twelve. Her mother, who was her only parent, had taken her own life after suffering from years of depression and Buddhist monks at a nearby monastery had adopted Kamiko. She cleaned and cooked for the monks until the head of the monastery saw something special about her and took her under his wing. During which time she became a devout Buddhist herself and studied dhyāna. This was the training of the mind, which leads to a state of perfect awareness. She had left the monastery when she was twenty and travelled to various places around the world to further her studies. She said she had studied dhyāna to become aware of the suffering of others with mental problems and to try and help them. As she spoke, I could feel the energy that was coming from her change to frustration and sadness. I felt that she was carrying the unfounded guilt, from all those years ago, of not being able to help her mother. I sensed that she was even blaming herself for her mother's illness and the desire to help others was a way of correcting the wrongdoing that she thought she had done.

I told her my story, starting from when Charlie died, and although she was obviously intrigued, I saw there was doubt in her eyes about what I was able to sense and communicate. Although she believed that I sensed her energy before I saw her, my other experiences must have sounded a little far-fetched to say the least. Unlike the captain of the boat that took me to Shanghai, who genuinely believed my every word, I could see that she was questioning what I was now capable of.

I put my recent life story on pause and said, *"You don't believe me."*
"I didn't say that," she answered, *"I know you can sense the energy of living things but what you've just told me sounds so fantastic."*
"So do you believe that I can sense the energy of the cat that is creeping up on the sparrow behind me?"
She looked over my shoulder at the cat and bird behind me. Her eyes widened as she said, *"er, yes I do now."*
"But do you believe that I can change the cat's mind?"
"What do you mean?"

I wasn't sure I could do what I was about to attempt but I presumed that if I could communicate, by thought, with a brutal Brooklyn gang who were on the verge of killing me, an old moggy shouldn't prove too difficult to persuade to change its plans. I closed my eyes and concentrated on the cat's hunting instinct. Almost instantly the cat stopped its stalking, looked around then turned and walked away from the bird.

Kamiko stood up and froze for a few seconds before saying:

"Oh, oh. I am so sorry…I do believe you. That's incredible."

She sat back down beside me and said, *"If you can do that, you can do so much more."*
"So I'm beginning to find out," I replied. *"You obviously have something in mind?"*
Her voice went into a slightly higher pitch as she said, *"every forty seconds someone in the world takes their own life."*
"And you want me to stop that from happening?"
"I know that sounds impossible," she quickly answered, *"but you could at least make a difference…surely."*

I held both of her hands and looked so deeply into her eyes I saw a tiny blood vessel burst with excitement next to one of her large, dark brown pupils.
"Before we go any further with this notion you have got to stop blaming yourself for what happened to your mother."
"I don't blame myself." she snapped.
"Really?"
Through a flood of tears Kamiko tried, as best she could, to explain.

"Mama was a poet. She had lots of books published. Then when I was born she stopped writing. She would just cry all of the time. One day Papa left and didn't come back. Mama would cry even more. Then one day when I came home from school she was lying on the bed with empty bottles of pills next to her. I called an ambulance but she was dead. If I hadn't been born she would have stayed happy but because I made her so unhappy the only thing she could do to punish me was to kill herself."

"No it wasn't," I said as I held her hands tighter. *"She had an illness that was way beyond anything you could have done, and even if you hadn't been born, she would have had another child and she would have experienced the same feelings of depression."*

Kamiko nodded, a little unconvincingly.

I continued to try and convince her that her mother's death wasn't her fault. *"After Charlie died I had nothing or no one to carry on living for and that day when I went to the coast was going to be my last day. I went to the cliff top to jump off but fate had other ideas. I sat on that bench and met David and he said six words that gave me hope, "you can still talk to her." That was all I needed to carry on. I had a project, a belief that my life would change. Your mother also had a project, and that project was 'project suicide' that was what she had decided to do and nothing was going to stop her in the same way nothing was going to stop me from talking to Charlie again, even though I didn't know what David meant...and still don't really know but it was enough to convince me to carry on. I was determined to find Charlie again in the same way that your mother was determined to end her life, which had become meaningless to her. It was the strongest motivation that she had, and it was nothing to do with you."*

Kamiko kissed my hand. *"Thank you."*
We sat and just looked at each other for a few minutes until she said, *"Can we give people who have the same project as mama something else to believe in? Can we change their minds?"*

I knew this was going to be a huge mountain to climb and I didn't feel that Saaya was leading the way or even giving me a leg up to

attempt it, but how could I refuse after everything that I had said to Kamiko? I also felt that, maybe, I was falling in love with her. But the tasks ahead meant that I would have to invade the minds of people who were intent on ending their lives and then give them an alternative direction to take. I wasn't sure that I would be able to withstand such pain. I couldn't help thinking that I had come so far and I wasn't sure that this task was supposed to be on my to do list but Kamiko interrupted my thoughts.
"I can take you to someone who needs help."

Next stop Bellevue Hospital. On the way there Kamiko told me we were going to see a young woman of twenty-four, which was the same age that Charlie would have been if she had lived. This was the first problem that I was going to have to face. Kamiko said the patient's name was Debbie, a suicide attempter who had cut her wrists but was discovered by her flat mate just in time to save her life. Before we went into Debbie's room we spoke to one of the nurses. Debbie appeared to be receiving the best treatment that was available at the hospital, which was a combination of stress suppressing drugs and therapy based on 'it's OK not to feel OK'. Obviously, none of which were working.

At first Debbie didn't resemble Charlie in any shape or form. She was a very tall young woman with striking red hair, which was a bit unkempt. She was sitting in her room, dressed in a white gown, gazing out of a barred window and didn't acknowledge us in any way when we entered.
Kamiko called to her, "Debbie this is Tim – he's come to talk to you."
There was a short pause before Debbie turned towards us.
"Not another fucking shrink?"
"No," I said *"and I haven't come to talk to you – you're going to talk to me."*
"Just fuck off. There, I've talked to you." She turned back to look out of the window.
"Just look at me," I said, *"that's all you have to do."*
Debbie turned back to face me. *"Alright Dim, that is your name isn't it? There, I'm looking at you. Now what?"*
"You don't have to speak to talk, I'll be able to hear you."
Debbie gave a forced laugh and replied, *"Oh great, that's all I need, a fucking fruitcake."*

It wasn't long before I could feel what she was going through. Pain isn't the right word to describe it. It was more like determination, but it was a resolution that was as negative as I've ever thought possible to experience. Everything other than wanting to leave this world was absent. It made me realise that no one, including doctors, haven't got a hope of comprehending the magnitude of such determination without personally experiencing it. I had never felt such a single-minded force of energy. I knew this was going to be a huge task.

I wanted to try and understand how she had become the way she was. I needed to probe back into her childhood to see what contributed to her state of mind and what triggered her tragic mental condition. What I was expecting to discover turned out to be the complete opposite of what I did see. I thought I would see her traumatised by parents who were cruel or ill themselves but all I could discern were the sort of loving ideal parents devastated and blaming themselves for their daughter's illness.

The more I shared her imprisoned mind the more I realised what a cancer it was – growing and invading until it had complete control over any logical and creative thought. She was her own captor trapped in a dark world. I wasn't fond of the expression, 'they were born that way' as I had always believed anyone could change their situation, but I was starting to think that something may be present in her that was dominating her destiny. But what could be so determined to want to destroy its own life without any rational reason? The more I saw, the more contagious I felt it was becoming. I started to surrender to it. Whatever had dominated Debbie's mind was taking over mine. It was like falling under a bizarre sort of spell. If this could be rechannelled into a more positive intention the result would be phenomenal. I managed to resist the powerful urge to give in to it and, instead, tried to understand why this was happening to Debbie and now me.

And then I realised what it was and how it started. It was a seed – a seed of doubt that had been planted a long time ago. Like a weed, it had been allowed to grow, flourish and overpower anything beautiful around it. I went deeper into Debbie's memory. She was in her mid-teens and very happy. It was then that I discovered a similarity to Charlie. Debbie loved animals. She had that same look on her face that Charlie had when she was surrounded by them. I felt a sharp pain in my chest but I knew I had to carry on. Debbie was working in an animal rescue charity during her school holidays. One evening the rest of the staff had left and she was on her own. She loved having all the animals to herself. There was a loud bang on the door. She answered it to find a man holding a dog covered in blood. It had been hit by a truck and was in a bad state. Debbie frantically tried to contact a vet to come out but no one was available so she took the dog's life into her own hands. I saw the tears in her eyes as I replayed her memory of that evening. She did everything she could from cleaning the wounds to covering it with a blanket, but the dog's breathing was getting shallow and its body was trembling. She looked at its hopeless fight for life and made the only decision she thought she could. She remembered a vet injecting adrenalin into a dog to stimulate its heart so that's what she did. As she stood back to wait for a result the dog's eyes opened wide, then it died. She was convinced that she had killed the dog and that's when the seed started to grow. From that day on she felt useless. She found homes for the pets that she had through fear of hurting them. She didn't trust herself and that feeling amplified until she was convinced that she didn't deserve to live. And all because of a mistake that she thought she had made. The seed that had grown in her head was determined to suffocate her and she had become too weak to fight it. She was left with the one burning ambition that would free her from her torment – ending her life.

My first thought was how can anyone be driven to such despair about the death of a dog? But that wasn't the point; it was just a trigger that activated a dangerous characteristic that was lurking and waiting for the ideal moment to take over. Unlike Kamiko's guilt that developed into a Buddhist following, Debbie's guilt gave birth to her own potential destruction.

A reasonable and logical therapy would have been to take her out of her self-inflicted prison and remind her of the beautiful world around her. Flowers, birds, the feeling of summer rain on her face, and get her back in touch with the animals that she loved. But this would only have rubbed salt in the wound and convinced her even more that she didn't deserve any of it.

It was then that I decided to tell her a lie.

To first gain her trust and belief I spoke to her the way I spoke to Shelly on the train. *"Debbie I know about the dog that died and what that day meant to you."*
She looked at me startled. *"How did you do that? How did I hear your voice in my head when you didn't say anything?"*
I stopped talking telepathically and continued to speak normally.
"You have just shared your memories with me. Do you believe me?"
"Why should I?" she answered. *"It must be some sort of trick. If you can really read my mind, tell me the name of the cat I had when I was seven."*
"Crackers, you called it crackers because it used to do crazy things."
Debbie sat back in her chair. *"Shit, that is freaky."*
"So now you believe me?" I said.
"Yes, yes...OK I believe you."

233

It was then that I told the lie.
"Then believe this. I am able to recall and know everything that happened on that day. The dog died a few seconds before you injected it. The reaction that you saw was a last nervous response to its system shutting down."
She burst out crying. *"I didn't kill it?"*
"No, in fact you gave it its last moment of comfort, which was all you, or anyone else, could have done."
Of course, I had no way of getting into the dead dogs head but by now I had won Debbie's trust and abusing it seemed the best way forward.
She started laughing quite uncontrollably until eventually, she was silent and then said, *"My God, I could have gone on to be a vet. What a waste of all those years. How did I get into such a fucking state? Now what do I do?"*
"Not try to kill yourself?" I asked.
"Yeah, as well as that?" she laughed again.
Kamiko stepped forward, put her arms around Debbie and said,
"Welcome back."

After a few more tears and nervous laughter I looked again into Debbie's eyes and told her

"Because of what you've experienced you are in a very special position to save a lot of lives."

"What do you mean?" she asked.

"No one is more qualified than you to understand the overpowering feeling to destroy your own life. Psychiatrists and psychologists can only partly understand the destructive motivation that can dominate the mind but you have actually been in that war zone and won the battle. You have felt what other people in the same position are feeling and with that knowledge you can help them to achieve what you have."

And that's exactly what she did. But it wasn't without a lot of involvement from Kamiko and me.

Chapter 4

Kamiko and Debbie set up a counselling clinic at the Mahayana Buddhist Temple and the news got around quite quickly to relatives of, mainly, young people who had found themselves in desperate situations.

Reluctantly they would turn up suspicious and disbelieving and most of them expressing their views of not wanting to talk to me. Despite Kamiko and Debbie having done some of the groundwork, telling them how I had managed to turn their lives around, the meetings didn't often get off to a good start. Most of them had made up their minds that they didn't want to be part of this world and I was seen as just another shrink that didn't understand.

The first meeting was with a young Puerto Rican guy in his early twenties. To say he was screwed up would have been an understatement and it wasn't difficult to understand why he had got himself into the situation that he had. He was from East Harlem, known as Spanish Harlem and was the son of a professional boxer. His mother had died giving birth to him so he had a tough task ahead from day one, especially because he was gay – something his father didn't want to accept or know about. All this I was told by Debbie before I even met the young man called Jorge.

He lived in a tough area and rather than learn to stand up for himself like his father wanted him to, he would get beaten up regularly by the neighbourhood homophobes. Despite his father insisting on giving him boxing lessons Jorge would just turn the other cheek and get the crap beaten out of him. Every time he walked down his own street, it was like entering the wolf enclosure at Central Park Zoo. His Dad had got him a job at a warehouse on Harlem River where he would continually get the piss taken out of him.

After a lot of resistance, eventually Jorge allowed me to connect with his thoughts. I was hoping to discover a hidden 'Billy Elliot' type of talent or even a potential musician or painter but there was nothing to build on. Jorge was just a young man, with no particular interests, who hated being continually pressured to become someone he wasn't and this had driven him to want to stop being alive. I was faced with a difficult problem - where could I go from here?

The more I shared his mind the more I became aware of something that was tormenting Jorge. It centred around a place that he would regularly visit to enable him to be who he really wanted to be, if only for a few hours a week. 8th Avenue Chelsea, a popular gay area of Manhattan. But he knew if he told his Dad about his desire to live there it would be the end of their relationship and Jorge didn't have the heart to do that. The sad reality of the feelings of suicide is the powerful belief that it is not only right for who is experiencing it but it's also best for the loved ones of the person who has decided to end their life. Far from selfishness the person who is driven to his or her own finality sees it as an act of ultimate selflessness.

So, I arranged with Debbie to meet Jorge's father. He lived in a small apartment above a drug store on the junction of 125th Street and Lexington Avenue - one of the worst areas of East Harlem. Shootings, stabbings and armed robberies were as common as lentils in a vegan kitchen. We arrived just as a squad car was carting off a couple of dubious looking characters in handcuffs who were being cheered by a gathering of the on-looking neighbourhood.

The cruel and heartless man I thought I was going to meet turned out to be the complete opposite of what I was expecting. He was a tough looking character for sure, but he was incredibly polite and welcoming. I locked into his thoughts and personality straight away and realised that he didn't hate or was embarrassed by his son. In fact, I sensed the incredible love and protective energy he had for Jorge.

I didn't tell him what I was capable of, as I didn't want him to think I was some kind of weirdo, so I just listened and spoke normally, which lasted for well over an hour. The incredible thing about this man was throughout the whole conversation I knew he was crying inside but he didn't show it at all. He had learned how to control his emotions through his fear of implying a kind of weakness that he didn't want anyone to see. His sole purpose in life was to make sure that Jorge would be OK. He was all he had, and every time he looked at his son he vowed to the memory of his wife that Jorge would be protected. That was the reason for the boxing lessons and the strict relationship. The problem was that it wasn't seen that way by Jorge – he felt trapped, unloved and misunderstood. It was also made more difficult for him living in such a tough area where sympathy and understanding for Jorge's sexuality was virtually absent and in that part of the city what wasn't understood was seen as a threat and destroyed. No wonder Jorge's life had become unbearable. Sadly, Dad was also hanging on to the notion that Jorge would grow out of being gay. There was only one way out for Jorge and that was not to have to suffer this torment, which meant ending his miserable life.

Debbie's contribution was invaluable to stopping this from happening and together we hatched a plan. She would take on the Jorge challenge and I would handle Dad. The first thing I had to do was take him on a bit of a trip to where he would never have dreamt of visiting - 8th Avenue Chelsea. It was obvious at first that he didn't feel at ease walking through an area where same sex couples were holding hands and outwardly showing their affection for each other, but when a few of them said hello he started to relax a little. Fortunately, he didn't realise that they assumed we were a couple.

The reason I took him there was to show him where Jorge could be safe, happy and most important of all, have a reason to live, instead of being the prisoner of the person who loved him the most. We sat on a bench in Chelsea Park and after a few quiet minutes Dad opened up. He pointed to a couple of teenage girls laughing and playing with a dog.

"Why can't he find a nice girl like that?"
"Because if he did he would be lying to himself," I answered.
"He didn't wake up one morning and decide to be gay."
"But it's not natural," he said with a fair amount of conviction.
"It's as natural to him as being straight is to you," I said.
"Straight? Straight?" Is that what we are. Another word for dull?
"Gay people don't think you're dull, they just accept you for what you are unlike a lot of straight people who don't accept them for what they are."
"So are you gay too?" he asked.
"No, so you don't have to sit that far away from me." I laughed.
He smiled and sat in silence for a while before saying:
"So what do I do, just let him go?"
"It's not as simple as that." I said. *"He'll just think you're giving up on him."*

"*Well I am ain't I?*"
"*Have you ever told him you love him?*" I asked.
"*Course I ain't,* Dads don't say that to sons."
"*Oh yes they do.*"
"*Well this Dad don't...especially the way he is.*"
"*Why, are you concerned that he might think you're coming on to him?*"
"*Well, you don't know,*" he said.
"*I do and I can assure you he won't.*"
"*So, you want me to say I love you to a faggot?*"
"*No I want you to say I love you to your son. That's of course if you do love him.*"
"*Of course I fucking do.*"
"*Then say it.*"
"*OK, I love Jorge.*"
"*Not to me, to him.*"
"*Ah shit – what good will it do?*"
"*It may stop him from killing himself.*"

Dad stood up and looked at me. His hands were shaking.
"*What?*"
"*It's time to tell you what I know.*" I confessed.
"*What do you know?*" he asked.

242

"That I can share people's minds. I know what they are thinking and what troubles them and I know that Jorge isn't in a good place right now. He wants to end his life."
Dad's response was more or less what I expected.
"Horse shit…why should I believe that?"
Here we go again I thought – time to prove myself.
"OK, just think of your earliest memory of Jorge."

I didn't have to wait long to see what he was seeing. He was holding the baby Jorge next to a bed. A doctor was looking up at him and shaking his head as Jorge's mother lie dead. He then took Jorge and went outside and just walked for miles crying and kissing his baby. I told him what I had seen.
"How the fuck? No one knew that…no one."
He sat back down and put his head in his hands.
"Will you help him? Will you help me?"
"Yes, that's why I'm here, to help you help each other."

In the distance two figures were approaching. I knew who they were before Dad realised. It was Jorge and Debbie.
"Hey that's Jorge isn't it? Who's he with?" asked Dad.
"Her name is Debbie and don't get your hopes up – she's not his girlfriend."
Debbie and I left Jorge and his dad to it but as we got about 100 yards away I couldn't resist doing a long distance eavesdrop, thanks to Amar's training.
"Hi Dad," said Jorge.
"Hi son, how are ya?"
"OK, what are you doin' here?"
"Waitin' for you I guess."
There was then a slight pause as Dad did a bit of shuffling around before nervously saying,
"You know I love ya son?"
"Love you too Dad but are you OK with what I am?"
"You're my boy, that's what you are. That's all that counts."
"Thanks Dad, that means a lot. Can I hug ya?"
"Guess so…no one's gonna give a damn 'bout two guys huggin' round here."
Debbie jumped up and down with excitement.
"Look, look they're hugging."

244

Dad continued. *"So, we better get you out of Harlem and find you a place around here somewhere."*
"But what about you?" asked Jorge.
"I'll come visit at weekends."
"And what if I meet someone. Would you be OK with that?"
"One extra faggot's not gonna get me dumb tight."
Fortunately, this made Jorge laugh.
"So, no more boxing lessons Dad?"
"No more boxin' kid. Now we better find you a job round here."
"Yeah...let's do that but not in a warehouse or anything like that"
"Sure, you can be a waitress or something."
"You mean waiter Dad."
"Yeah right, a waiter."

The last I heard of Jorge he didn't become a waiter; he got a job at a recording studio as a runner and went on to become one of the best sound engineers in New York where he met Michael, the love of his life. As for Dad, he loved having two sons to goad.

As the months went by Kamiko and I became closer. We were hardly away from each other, and it was good to see her confidence grow as she became involved with her work at the clinic. We were a good team helping young people to change and deal with their lives. Every day was a different challenge, but they were all rewarding. Although she tried to hide it, I could sense that her feelings for me were mirroring my attraction to her and the more I could sense it the more aroused and frustrated I became. Then one very hot summer afternoon the inevitable happened. We were sitting in her room sipping iced jasmine tea and fanning ourselves with magazines. The heat was making her thin cotton robe stick to her. She looked down at herself and then at me. I immediately sensed what she was thinking. She was going to take the top off – surely not, I thought. I must have got it wrong, but my senses were spot on and she did take it off revealing no other clothing underneath.

She just sat there for almost a whole minute, which seemed like an hour, allowing me to look at everything that had been hidden for so long. I had often imagined how she would look without that robe but reality far exceeded anything imagination suggested. The rest of the afternoon was spent – well… best you use your own imagination as my words won't even come close to expressing how sensational that day and every afternoon for the next year was. If this was what I was destined to be led to then the previous seven years was worth the wait, but I knew that wasn't how my future was going to be. Saaya, my guardian, had been quiet for the last two years but he was about to end my sabbatical. I was getting strong feelings to move on but my love for Kamiko and the thought of losing her was conflicting with what I knew I really would have to do. Every time the thought of leaving entered my mind I would fight it, sometimes I even tried to shout out loud *"stop it, go away"* but I knew I would have to obey soon. Then one day Kamiko made it easier for me to surrender to fate.

One crisp November morning we were walking in Washington Square Park, one of my favourite places in New York. There were always musicians performing for free, from terrific guitarists to amazing sax players. The energy that was dominant was peace and contentment, although that wasn't what I was picking up from Kamiko. I knew what she was going to ask before she asked it and I knew my answer was going to be difficult.

"Do you always know what's in my head?" she said.
"Why are you asking me that?"
"Because I need to know if every thought that I have becomes your thought too, or do you just tune in when you want to."
I tried to make fun of it. *"If I was constantly aware of everything that was going through your deep and complex head I would be permanently fucking exhausted."*
She didn't appreciate the joke and continued to probe.
"But if I have a strong feeling about something, will you automatically pick it up?"
Suddenly this wasn't like the Kamiko I knew and loved. It wasn't just the questions she was asking that were worrying me it was the overpowering concern that I sensed she had.

"OK," she continued as she stopped walking and gave me an aggressive and challenging look. *"What am I thinking now?"*
She was testing me and I knew, after quite a long pause, it was time for me to be honest with her.

"You're thinking that the guy behind me is pretty hot...but you don't really believe that – in fact you don't fancy him at all." I thought being totally honest would put her concerns, that she obviously had, to rest but it had the opposite affect.
"Shit, that's worse than I thought," she said. *"I can't even think a lie."*
"But why would you want to?"
Tears started to fill her eyes. *"Because there are times when you do something that pisses me off, which isn't really important, and not worth mentioning but it freaks me out to think that you know every thought that I have. I'm sure I piss you off sometimes, it's natural. We can't live in a loved-up bubble twenty-four hours a day and I know you realise that too but sometimes I feel that I'm walking on eggshells. It's like my thoughts are being bugged and there's nothing we can do about it."*

I sensed how difficult it was for her to say what she was thinking, at that moment, so I made it easier for her.
"So when are you going back to Japan?"
"Soon...Oh Tim I so wish it didn't have to end. I love you so much and it's because of you that

I've been able to help people and change my life to give it meaning over the last two years but I can't live like this."

I held her and whispered through her jet-black hair, *"I know you can't. I supposed I thought that you might get used to being with a weirdo."* I felt her sob and pulled her closer. *"And I know that you really do love me and this isn't just an excuse to go."*
Kamiko looked up at me. *"What am I thinking now?"*
"You're thinking that you want to go home and fuck."
"Correct...as usual."

Chapter 5

The day Kamiko left I gave in to what Saaya was, by now, desperately trying to tell me. At first, I thought I was being lured back to India, which I certainly didn't have a problem with, but the feeling I was getting soon became clearer. It was a different continent entirely. I was to head south to Venezuela, the most dangerous country, not only in South America but the world. It seemed pretty obvious that I was going to come up against either murders, kidnapping, armed robbery or all of the above. After a six-hour flight I landed at Maiquetia International Airport in Caracas, the most violent city in Venezuela. As soon as I got there my, so-called, guardian directed me to where I was supposed to go. It was called Catia - the worst barrio in the city.

So, there I was, in the worst area of the most violent city of the most dangerous country on the planet – thanks Saaya.

I still had my Buddhist's hairstyle, in other words bald, and was wearing purposely chosen scruffy clothes so the prospect of being robbed or kidnapped was pretty low as I made my way through the surreal backstreets. Looking up to lower than rooftop height was a mass of electric cables like a spider's web of live voltage that would have given an electrician from the western world recurring nightmares.

Every window was barred with makeshift scrap metal variations in desperate attempts to protect whoever was inside and to signal the threatening outside world to stay away. The odd burnt out car blocked the already narrow streets and emaciated dogs scavenged and fought for discarded food, too rotten for human consumption, in filthy gutters. Angry anti-authoritarian graffiti was aggressively sprayed or painted on every available space from walls to boarded-up doors and corrugated fences. You didn't need to have my heightened senses to feel the tension that was all around.

As Saaya guided me through the compendium of poverty I started to lock on to a strong energy of children up ahead. I had no further need for my guide – I knew exactly where I was going and had a feeling that the experience about to be revealed was to be far from pleasant. At first, I thought I was heading for a school but I had sensed kids in schools before and the overriding vibe had been of excitement, fun and friendship. This was different, there was none of that. What I was picking up was fear and, most strongly of all, confusion.

After about a hundred more yards I came to the end of an alleyway. There was a large door with thick black paint flaking off it. I stood for a while and listened. All I could hear from the other side of the door was breathing; the shallow, nervous breaths of around fifty or more children. I tried to push open the door but it was locked. I then heard a man's harsh voice *"Tomaré estos tres por 50 bolívares cada uno."* (I'll take these three for 50 bolivars each). I sensed a struggle as three of the tiny breaths quickened. I felt them being separated from the other children. I didn't need to see what I knew was happening behind that door. Children were being sold for whatever the buyer wanted them for. I felt sick and enraged. If I had allowed impulse to take control I would have beaten down the door but that would only have resulted in a bullet in the head. I had to be smarter than that.

I had an idea. This country was highly religious and fearful of upsetting the Father, Son and Holy Spirit in any shape or form, so I decided to try and play the Catholic card. I knocked forcefully on the door and after a few seconds it was partially opened by a terrifying looking character. He had barely any skin that wasn't covered with aggressive looking tattoos – everything from tarantulas to skulls, and fortunately for me there was the head of Christ with a crown of thorns emblazoned on his bare chest.

"¿Qué deseas?" (What do you want?") He barked.

I stood and looked at him without saying a word. Then in my best schoolboy Spanish I communicated telepathically as I invaded his mind. I looked deeply into his eyes as my thoughts went into his head. I told him that he was committing a sin to Jesus by hurting the children and he must release them. I then took my best shot. I put my thoughts into the minds of three of the children to tell them to come and stand by me to be safe. One by one they came over and stood beside me. The smallest little girl reached out and held my hand.

I thought the man's jaw was going to hit the ground. His eyes bulged with amazement and terror. He was frozen in silence for a while then said in a trembling voice. *"e sub angel."* (It's an angel")

I then looked at the man buying the children – a slimy looking character with long greasy hair and wearing a shiny 80's looking suit. I told him the same thing, which caused him to stare at the tattooed ogre before running out of the door screaming with fear. The tattooed jailer backed off and spoke through trembling lips, *"Tomarlas, tomarlas."* ("Take them, take them.")

So, there I was walking through the streets of Caracas, like the pied piper without a flute, followed by fifty-four children. It was a strange but wonderful feeling. At first I had no idea where I was going but after about a mile an old man appeared from one of the run-down houses. *"Follow me, quick, follow me."* He said running off down a narrow alleyway. With nothing to lose except my life, all fifty-five of us followed him. For an old guy he was as nimble as a whippet snaking his way through the maze of dilapidated surroundings. I picked up the smallest child and broke into a jog, checking to see if all of the kids were with me. Very soon we came to a small town square. The old man was standing by a beaten up old bus. His English wasn't great but good enough to be understood. He opened the door to the bus and pointed to the inside. *"Get in, get in...they will be safe soon."*

He drove us for about an hour – out of the city heading west through open countryside. His driving was about as good as his English, so I was relieved when we reached our final destination. It was a children's charity village; not exactly a Shangri-La but a safe haven compared to where we had come from. Two young women appeared and obviously knew the old man as one of them said, *"Hola José."* What followed was a lot of shoulder shrugging from all three of them. I could sense that they were all a little confused, to say the least about who I was and how I had come to be in possession of a bus load of children. Eventually one of the women approached me. I decided that the best explanation to give was not to tell the whole truth, so I said that I had broken into a building where I saw children being taken earlier, and escaped with them while their captor was out. This seemed to go down OK and I was welcomed, fed and watered.

The place felt bizarre. Animal sanctuaries are commonplace but the thought of a similar setup for children shocked and upset me. Establishments like that shouldn't have to exist. The old man, José as I now knew him, offered me a ride back to the city. I thought about going back and pulling the angel stunt again but I thought that would be pushing my luck, so as Saaya wasn't willing me to move on I decided to stay for a while. I wanted to see the children settle in and maybe help out wherever I could, so I asked the manager of the village if that was OK. She jumped at the offer and I stayed for a few months teaching English.

It wasn't long before I had a nickname. The musical Annie was one of the children's favourite films played on an ancient looking tape machine at least once a week and because of my shaved head I became Daddy Warbucks, which appealed to me. I was going to let my hair grow but when I was given that name I decided to keep shaving.

Being amongst children was like a breath of fresh air. As well as the reward of seeing them change to become happier and grow in confidence, I also realised that their innocence and simple outlook to life was both eye and mind opening. Sometimes, in between lessons, I would sit outside under the shade of an Araguaney tree and lock-in to their individual thoughts. Their uncomplicated appreciation of life was humbling. If they were kicking a ball around or playing their version of baseball that was the only thing they were thinking about. Not a single worry or distraction ever came into their thoughts. People take years to empty their minds to be able to meditate with any beneficial affect but here were kids, some of them as young as four, who were able to free their minds of anything other than what they wanted to think about. Back in the days before I discovered India, and what Amar taught me, I would find it impossible to free myself from concerns and irrelevant thoughts. I felt thankful for now being able to do what these children could do naturally. This was my most treasured part of the day to just sit and share what they could do. The only difference was they just took it for granted but I never did. It didn't occur to me that someone was about to see into my mind too.

It was during a particularly hot afternoon as I was enjoying some well-earned me-time after the children had gone indoors for their last meal of the day. I started to meditate and found that almost instantly I was able to free my mind and enter a state of complete tranquility. After a few minutes I felt someone was trying to make contact with me. It was an energy that I hadn't experienced before. At first I thought it was an animal as it was so pure but I soon realised it was a child, but unlike any of the children that were in the village. I opened my eyes and saw a young girl of about twelve looking at me from some distance away. I had never seen such a tall child that young before. She must have been over six foot.

We spoke, from the same distance, through thought without speaking out loud, in a language neither Spanish nor English but in a way we could both understand. The first thing she asked was *"are you like me? Can you hear me?"*
"Yes," I answered, *"I can hear you."*
She then turned around and ran into the main building. I wanted to go after her but thought it best to wait until she was ready to communicate again. I asked one of the staff who the new girl was. She told me that the girl had been left outside. An old pickup truck had

stopped by the gate and someone had let her out. There was a note in her hand asking to be cared for as her grandmother couldn't afford to look after her and she didn't want her to be sold. The note ended with, *"her name is Valeria and she is a very special girl."* She certainly was, as I was soon to find out.

The process of getting to know Valeria was slow. She was shy and seemed frightened of her own power, but I was desperate to know more about her. It had taken me a decade to reach my level of awareness and ability and here was a child who was able to do the same. Was she taught from a baby or was she born with the gift? I had to find out. During the following few weeks we would communicate, by telepathy, in bite sized chunks from a respectable distance. None of the questions I asked at first were too taxing for her – just things like what's your favourite colour and food. Eventually I gained her trust and the questions became a little more probing, but I still couldn't unearth why she could do what she could because she just didn't know. I tried a non-telepathic approach and actually spoke to her but she clearly couldn't speak any English so what we were doing was incredible

- to be able to communicate without a common language. My thoughts were in English and hers were in Spanish but somehow we both understood each other completely as long as we didn't actually speak. Sometimes we would play games. She would love playing 'guess the animal I'm thinking of'. I would make her laugh by thinking things like, what has fur, four paws with claws, makes a meow noise and is coloured pink with blue spots? She would look confused and answer that she didn't know. I would tell her that it was a blue and pink spotted cat. She soon got the hang of my bad jokes and would join in with some of her own. My favourite was: what's long, thin, bites and has fifty legs? When I gave up guessing she told me it was a snake and she lied about the legs. I didn't have the heart to tell her I knew that was what she was thinking.

In between the fun and games I would try and probe a little deeper into her past but there wasn't much to discover except she had lived in the same small, one room apartment all her life. She never knew her parents and her grandmother, who brought her up and never spoke of them. Then one day I discovered a lot more about Valeria.

It was one late afternoon when school had finished for the day. I was sitting in my usual shady spot when I heard a beautiful voice singing in Hindi.

इस धरती पर मैं फिर से आता हूं,
बोधगया में मेरा घर है।
प्रत्येक यात्रा जो मैं लेता हूं,
प्रत्येक शरीर जो मेरा अपना है,
मुझे ज्ञान और सीख देगा
अगले जीवन के लिए।
इस बार विद्वान होने के लिए,
पहले जैसा योद्धा नहीं।
मेरे नए अस्तित्व को परिष्कृत करने के लिए
और मेरे संसार को जारी रखो।
एक महिला का रूप अब मेरा है
दूसरों को जीवन देने के लिए।
मैं उनके लिए अच्छे कर्म की कामना करता हूं
दुनिया को शांति देने के लिए।
मेरी यात्रा जारी है।
मेरा नाम सुषमा है।

I couldn't believe that I was hearing a language that was nearly ten thousand miles away from India.
Roughly translated the words were:

*On this earth I arrive again,
In Bodh Gaya to be my home.
Each journey that I take,
each body that I own,
will give me wisdom and learning
to take to the next life.
This time to be a scholar,
not a warrior like before.
To refine my new existence
and continue my Samsara.
A woman's form is now mine
to give life to others.
I wish for them to have good Karma
to give peace to the world.
My journey continues.
My name is Sushma.*

The source of the voice was even more amazing. Through an open window in the main hall of the building I saw it was coming from Valeria. She sensed I was there and stopped singing and smiled at me. As we joined in thought I told her she had a beautiful voice and asked how she could sing in Hindi. She replied that she didn't know what it was; it was something that she had always been able to do.

No one had taught it to her and not only was she unaware that she was singing in Hindi she also didn't know that she was singing about a woman called Sushma – the same name as David's grandmother. Could this be a coincidence or could it be that a few things were beginning to join up? There was another question I was asking myself: did I come to Venezuela to rescue children or was I destined to meet Valeria for some special reason? I needed to analyse that song further.

It was pretty obvious that it was about reincarnation – something I now totally believed in, but what I was more intrigued about was the mention of Bodh Gaya. This was a place I had heard about and was supposed to be the birth of Buddhism. It was also often referred to as India's spiritual capital. I meditated for the next four hours to try and clear my thoughts and seek whatever guidance I could from Saaya. The response was very strong. I had to go to Bodh Gaya where I knew answers were waiting to be revealed.

Before I left I communicated with Valeria to let her know where I was going, and I promised I would return to tell her what I would discover.

Chapter 6

Another air ticket bought and I was bound for Gaya. My inheritance from Dad was holding up well, in fact it had grown somewhat in size over the years of very little expenditure. I arrived feeling like I had never left. Even though I had never been to that part of India before, the familiar smells and colours seemed to welcome me home. At first I thought I was headed to where the giant statue of Buddha is, seated in a meditation pose and rising to over sixty feet high, or the Mahabodhi Temple, where the Buddha is said to have attained enlightenment but no. Saaya was guiding me to a remote small temple about ten miles away from all of this; isolated from the thousands of tourists and pilgrims that visited Gaya every year. From the airport I decided to set out on foot. The walk was only two hours; nothing compared to a few of my past treks across this beautiful country.

The temple I arrived at was understated and modest compared to the amazing architectural Buddhist structures that dominated the area. But this wasn't Buddhist; it was a Hindu temple dedicated to Saraswati, the goddess of knowledge, music, art and wisdom. It appeared to be the perfect link to Valeria and her captivating song.

There was no one around, not a priest or a worshipper in sight but there was a strong and familiar presence. I sat down on an old wooden seat and it wasn't long before I looked down and saw the odd socks of David sitting beside me.

"Welcome to Saraswati Temple Tim," he said casually.
"Hello David, fancy meeting you here."
I told him why I was there and about the song that Valeria had sung.
As I looked around at the cluttered collection of statues and faded paintings that adorned the

temple as David said: *"Ready for the next story?"*

"Well that's why I'm here so yes let's have it."

"My grandmother Sushma was born here. Her mother was found by the priest of the temple in the forest nearby. She was wandering in a state of semi-consciousness and pregnant with Sushma. The mother disappeared after giving birth and nothing was ever known about her or where she came from. Sushma was brought up by the childless wife of the priest. When Sushma was only four years old the priest heard her sing the song that you heard Valeria singing. No one had taught it to her and she became something of a mystic, so much so that people thought she was blessed. She was also seen to communicate with animals, befriending and talking to them in thought. Then one day, when Sushma had reached the age of seventeen a Maharaja was travelling north and heard about Sushma and considered her to be sent from the gods, a rare prize to own, so he married her and took her away with him. She never loved the Maharaja but remained a loyal wife, until she met Amar. The rest you know about."

David allowed a few seconds for me to process that bombshell before continuing: *"Samsara doesn't always occur immediately after someone passes on, it can take years before the spirit chooses another body to continue with."*
I asked the question that I knew would receive the obvious answer. *"So Valeria is the reincarnation of Sushma, your grandmother?"*
"Yes"
What I wasn't expecting was what David said next.
"And you will need to guide her in using her gift."

I thought it was going to be difficult enough convincing a twelve-year-old South American girl that she is the reincarnation of an Indian princess let alone how I was supposed to guide her through life, but David didn't leave me guessing for long.

"You already know that she has a beautiful voice. You and her together must use that voice to communicate to those who are able to hear songs that go beyond just words and melodies – music that sends powerful messages."

"But singers and composers have always attempted to do that."
"Attempted yes but succeeded no, because no singer has ever had the gift that Valeria has. Amongst her audiences there will be people who will hear more. They will sense her thoughts; the hidden messages that will spread like a pandemic of peace."
"And how will she do that?" I asked.
"You will teach her to think of things that matter while she is singing, that will help to create a better world – thoughts of unity, understanding and compassion for others. Not everyone will hear her thoughts but some will, and it will change their lives and they will pass it on to friends, family and anyone who wants to listen."
"What will she sing?" I asked.
"Songs that you will write." Came the reply. Although my copywriting skills weren't bad, song writing was a different task entirely. The closest I'd ever got to that was writing the occasional advertising jingles for things like fast food and fizzy drinks. But that was when I wasn't the person I had become, so why not give it a go I thought.

I returned to Venezuela and Valeria to tell her what I had discovered but I didn't want to do it through our unique telepathy. I thought it best to actually speak to her. After just a few weeks her English had become quite good, and we were able to have a reasonable conversation. I chose my moment carefully and waited for her reaction, which wasn't what I expected. She didn't run away or laugh. It was as if she was expecting to hear something along the lines of what I told her.

The songs I wrote were about everything that I had learned, and I thought mattered to the world - words about peace, harmony and love. They were OK but I thought they were nowhere near as good as what Dylan or Lennon had penned in the past, but when Valeria began to sing them they turned into something amazing. She gave them a meaning and a sound way beyond what I had written. I could sense what she was thinking as she was singing them and the impact was astounding. I was filled with hope and felt driven to tell the world. It wasn't my words that were doing this it was purely what Valeria turned them into – messages that were spiritual but without religion. The next stage was to see if an audience would feel the same.

The first venue was at a place called Los Guayos, a town near Lake Valencia just a few miles away. I wanted to start small to see what the reaction would be. I sensed mixed feelings in the local audience. Some were curious others were cynical. Valeria walked onto the modest size stage like a pro. Before she sang she put her hands together and said, *"Namaste,"* something I had never taught her, she just came out with it. The first song, which she sang in Spanish, was called 'Creer' (Believe) Silence fell for almost a whole minute when Valeria had finished, then the small audience burst into a rapturous applause as if it was from thousands of people.

As I looked around at the audience I could see that a few of the them weren't reacting in the same way as the others. They were just smiling; a couple of them had tears in their eyes. These were the people that David had said would hear more than just the song. They heard what Valeria was thinking. As each of them left they stopped by Valeria and said: *"Gracias."*

More and more concerts followed, playing to larger audiences as Valeria's popularity went from strength to strength and more people left the performances throughout South America taking Valeria's thoughts of peace with them. As news travelled further afield she started to get bookings to sing in countries throughout the world. By the time she turned sixteen world leaders, artists and heads of corporations were hearing her voice. Saaya was beginning to pull me in a different direction so it was time for me to leave Valeria with her faithful chaperone – one of the women from the children's charity village who had been with us since Valeria's first concert.

For the next three years Saaya guided me to a total of fourteen different countries throughout six of the world's continents, facing various challenges and doing whatever I could to stop suffering and ignorance. During this time I took a short break and went back to Paradip in India to see the captain who had, as well as given me free passage to Shanghai, become a good friend and I had promised I would return to tell him more of my story.

We spent three days together eating drinking and sharing our experiences. He had been studying yoga and meditation due, he said, to having met me. I was flattered at the thought of influencing such an intelligent man. Before we parted company he asked me again if he could write my story. I said I would be honoured. He told me he was going to call it The Gift.

Soon after leaving the captain and India I had an urge to go back to England. I was curious to know if I could settle into a new life, albeit a very different existence to what I had left behind before my incredible journey all those years ago. Attempting to pick up from where I had left off wasn't going to be an option though because as well as the prospect of my old job not being interesting to me anymore, I felt that I had a responsibility to continue to make a difference to things that mattered more than just doing a regular job.

The thought of returning to where I once lived in England didn't appeal to me either as there was nothing there for me to go back to. I didn't want to bump into anyone that I once knew and be confronted with explanations of why I had mysteriously disappeared all those years ago. I also didn't want to move to a city, or even a town, where I would be robbed of all the wonderful natural sounds and smells that had now become essential to my senses. I chose a tiny cottage near a place called Wasdale Head, a small hamlet in the Lake District. It overlooked Wastwater, the deepest lake in England. From there I planned to live out my days helping who I could without too much stress, which worked out fine for the first couple of years. I became a bit of a local hero locating and rescuing lost sheep and walkers from the wilds of Cumbria, but the days started to drag on and I began to feel as much use as a boy scout helping old ladies across the road. As beautiful as the place was, I knew I couldn't justify staying there when I was capable of achieving so much more.

Late one summer's evening I was sitting outside the cottage. It was unusually warm for that part of England with no hint of a breeze. I closed my eyes and listened for distant sounds. I could hear the powerful wings of a large bird of prey disturbing the still air high above me. I looked up and saw an osprey searching for its evening meal. I tried to meditate to be in perfect harmony with my surroundings, but Saaya was having none of it. My plan to settle down was about to come to an end. I was being drawn to somewhere in the Middle East. I wasn't sure where but I knew I had to leave the next day.

That was yesterday and I'm now on route to discover what my next quest is going to be, but before I do Saaya is guiding me to where all of this started - back to the clifftop where I first met David. I suppose I'm going to be told exactly where I'm going and why.

As I walk along the coastal path I can see the old bench in the distance.

So here I am, no sign of old odd socks though, just the salty smell of the early evening breeze from the sea. I <u>can</u> feel an energy, but it's not David.

"Namaste Dad."
"Charlie?"

Printed in Great Britain
by Amazon

35842795R00155